Stories to Share with My Partner

Book 13

Camden Books Publishing

José F. Nodar

Stories to Share with My Partner Book 13 / José F. Nodar
ISBN: 978-1-7643409-8-4 - Paperback
ISBN: 978-1-7643714-4-5 - E-Book

Dedication

In loving memory of my wife,

Miriam Vassallo Nodar,

and her enduring presence.

You are always in my thoughts.

For anyone who's ever loved deeply, lost fully, and still found

the courage to begin again.

Table of Contents

The Fall of the Camden Quills

The Camden Quills Writing Group had met every Thursday evening for seven years at the back of Northport Café & Bistro, where the coffee was strong, the muffins dry, and the opinions even drier.

The group was proud of its democratic spirit: everyone's work was treated equally, whether it was a sonnet, a crime thriller, or a tragic poem about a cat who ran away (and, sometimes, came back as a metaphor).

That was until "that blasted book."

The trouble began on a cool March evening when Marianne Doyle, a quiet widow known for her gentle short stories about lost umbrellas and elderly gardeners, arrived with a suspicious glint in her eye.

She was usually shy, the type of person who apologised to furniture when she bumped into it. But that evening she looked radiant.

Hair styled, lipstick bright, holding a book like a newborn.

"I have news," she said, with a tremor that made everyone look up from their caramel slices.

"Oh?" said Kevin Broome, the group's self-appointed literary expert, and resident cynic.

Kevin wrote "experimental fiction" that no one could finish, including Kevin. He once described his own work as "a conversation between philosophy and punctuation."

Marianne took a deep breath. "My novel, Winds of Desire, has just... well, it's been published. And—it's selling rather well."

There was a stunned silence.

Then, Claire, the retired librarian, clapped first.

"Oh, how wonderful! What's it about?"

Marianne blushed. "It's... um... a love story. Between a Scottish lighthouse keeper and an American botanist."

"Oh, so it's a romance," Kevin said, in the tone one might use for "a communicable disease."

"Well—yes," she admitted. "But there's history, emotion, longing—"

"And bodices?" Kevin interrupted.

"Don't tell me it's one of those books."

Claire gasped. "Kevin!"

Marianne smiled awkwardly. "It's... more emotional than steamy."

"Oh, please," Kevin said, leaning back in his chair. "Every romance author says that until you open to chapter seven and find someone's breeches in disarray."

By April, Winds of Desire had reached number three on the Australian bestseller list, sandwiched between a cookbook and a memoir by a cricket player who couldn't spell. The café owner even put a copy in the window, next to the specials board.

The rest of the Quills congratulated Marianne, except Kevin, who insisted it was all luck and marketing.

"She's being marketed, not published," he told the group one evening, waving his pen like a sword. "There's a difference between literature and emotional pap."

Claire rolled her eyes. "You're just jealous."

"Jealous? Of someone who writes about windswept love and moonlit glances?" he scoffed. "I write about existence itself!"

"Yes," muttered Tom, the group's resident poet, "and existence itself fell asleep halfway through your last story."

Kevin ignored him.

"Romance panders to the lowest common denominator. It's sugar for the brain."

Marianne, ever gracious, simply smiled.

"Well, sugar makes the tea sweeter, doesn't it?"

The jealousy soon turned creative.

Kevin announced he was writing a "meta-novel" called The Anatomy of a Cheap Love Story, which he described as "a deconstruction of romantic clichés in modern literature."

He claimed it wasn't about Marianne's book, merely inspired by "the phenomenon of sentimentality disguised as art."

The first reading didn't go well.

"The heroine," Kevin read, "was called Mary-Ann Dull, a widowed florist who thought love was like pruning roses— painful and repetitive."

Everyone squirmed.

Marianne sat still, expression unreadable.

"The hero," Kevin continued, "was a rugged lighthouse keeper named MacGuffin, whose only personality trait was the ability to stare broodily into the mist."

"Kevin!" Claire snapped. "That's clearly about Marianne's book."

Kevin pretended innocence.

"Is it? I just made it up. Perhaps she's projecting."

Tom coughed. "You literally said lighthouse keeper."

"Ah, but mine's symbolic," Kevin countered. "A metaphor for the false beacon of consumer-driven affection."

Marianne, to her credit, laughed softly.

"If you're going to parody me, at least make him a good kisser."

That got a round of laughter, but not from Kevin.

By May, the group had split into factions.

Half were "Team Marianne," who admired her success and secretly bought scented candles, hoping inspiration would strike.

The other half were "Team Literature," led by Kevin, who held late-night sessions at the pub to discuss the death of artistic integrity.

The Northport Café & Bistro became a battleground.

Marianne arrived one week later to find the specials board reading:

"Today's Soup: Jealousy Broth, Served Cold."

"Kevin," she said sweetly, "you didn't."

He sipped his long black. "Freedom of expression."

Things escalated further when Marianne appeared on a local radio show, describing the Quills as "a wonderful group of supportive writers."

Kevin nearly choked on his biscotti.

"Supportive? She's stolen my limelight! I discovered her!"

"No, you didn't," said Tom. "She joined two years before you."

"I mentored her," Kevin declared.

"You once told her to 'read more Kafka.'"

"Exactly!" Kevin said. "And look where it got her."

When Marianne's publisher announced a formal book signing at a local Camden bookshop, the Quills were invited.

Kevin refused.

"I will not attend an event that celebrates mediocrity."

But curiosity, and perhaps machismo, won.

He turned up late, wearing his "serious writer" outfit: black turtleneck, tweed jacket, and a scowl.

The place was packed.

Readers lined up with copies of Winds of Desire, whispering, and giggling. A few even wore fake kilts in honour of the hero.

Marianne sat behind a table, smiling as she signed.

Kevin hovered near the back, muttering to Tom.

"She's signing with hearts," he hissed. "Real authors sign with pens, not punctuation."

"Kevin," Tom said, "you're signing your own resignation from decency."

Unable to resist, Kevin approached the microphone during the Q&A session.

"I have a question," he bellowed. "Do you think mass appeal justifies literary compromise?"

The room fell silent.

Marianne blinked. "I'm not sure what you mean."

"I mean—does pandering to shallow desires count as art?"

A few audience members booed.

Someone yelled, "Get off the stage, mate!"

Marianne, calm as a saint, replied, "I think art is anything that connects with people's hearts. Even yours, if you still have one."

The crowd roared with laughter and applause.

Kevin turned crimson.

"You'll all see! Fads fade, but truth endures!"

Then he stormed out, accidentally knocking over a display of Winds of Desire on his way. Copies scattered like confetti. Someone filmed the whole thing. By the next morning, the clip titled "Angry Writer vs. Romance Queen" had 200,000 views.

After that, Kevin stopped attending the Quills.

He declared the group "spiritually bankrupt" and formed his own splinter cell: The True Pens Society (membership: one).

He even tried to hold meetings at the local library, but they told him solitary rants didn't count as community programs.

Meanwhile, the Camden Quills thrived.

Marianne's success drew new members, and local businesses sponsored an annual short-story prize in her name.

Kevin refused to enter, saying, "I don't compete in popularity contests."

But secretly, he was writing again, this time a "dark comedy" called The Lighthouse of Despair, about a misunderstood genius living among idiots.

One rainy afternoon, he spotted Marianne at the post office, chatting kindly with fans.

She saw him and waved.

"Kevin! How lovely to see you. How's your writing?"

He stiffened. "Profound. Possibly revolutionary."

"That's wonderful," she said warmly. "If you ever want feedback—"

"I don't need feedback," he interrupted. "My work speaks for itself."

"Does it speak to anyone else, though?" she teased gently.

He had no answer.

A month later, Kevin's bitterness reached volcanic levels when he found out Marianne's novel had been optioned for film.

"A movie! They'll probably cast someone named Chad in a fake accent!"

His only solace was the announcement that the group would read "anonymous excerpts" at the upcoming Writers' Festival.

Kevin saw his chance.

He submitted a piece titled "Love's Hollow Echo," supposedly an "objective satire." But everyone instantly recognised his style: sentences longer than paragraphs, footnotes attacking the concept of joy.

When Claire read it aloud at the festival, confusion spread.

"The heroine," she read slowly, "was a delusional scribbler whose success stemmed from the collective hormonal imbalance of her readers."

The audience murmured.

Claire frowned. "Kevin, is this—?"

He stood up. "Yes! And it's the truth! Someone has to expose the rot beneath the glitter!"

Marianne, sitting front row, whispered to Tom, "I think he's gone feral."

Kevin continued his tirade, declaring romance "the literary equivalent of instant noodles."

The audience booed.

Someone threw a program at him.

Eventually, security escorted him out, still shouting about "narrative integrity."

Weeks later, Kevin found himself alone again at Northport Café & Bistro.

The group had banned him, the internet had meme him ("Broody Writer vs. Lighthouse Lady"), and his own cat preferred the neighbour.

He ordered a flat white and sat in his usual corner.

From the radio, the host's voice chirped: "And now, the winner of this year's Camden Literary Prize... Kevin Broome, for The Lighthouse of Despair!"

He nearly dropped his cup.

Apparently, the judges had found his dark comedy "hilariously self-aware and touching." The local paper even called it "a brilliant satire on envy and ego."

He blinked.

They thought it was funny.

That evening, Marianne herself appeared at his table.

"Kevin," she said kindly, "congratulations. You won."

He gawked. "They—liked it?"

"They loved it. And so did I."

He frowned. "You read it?"

"Of course," she said. "It's sharp and honest, and yes, a little bitter, but very human. You just didn't realise you were writing about yourself."

He opened his mouth, then closed it.

For once, Kevin Broome was speechless.

Marianne smiled. "The group misses you. We're meeting next Thursday if you'd like to come."

He hesitated. "Wouldn't that be awkward?"

"Only if you compare me to instant noodles again."

Kevin snorted, and then, to his surprise, laughed. "All right. But no hugging."

The following Thursday, Kevin arrived early.

The others looked surprised but nodded politely.

Tom whispered, "If he bites, I'm leaving."

Kevin sat quietly as Marianne read an excerpt from her new book, Tides of Tomorrow. When she finished, everyone clapped. Kevin raised his hand.

"Yes, Kevin?" she asked, cautious.

"I just wanted to say..." He swallowed. "It's well-written."

The group stared.

"I mean, it's still romantic nonsense," he added quickly, "but the sentences are decent."

Marianne beamed.

"Thank you, Kevin. Coming from you, that's almost affectionate."

He grumbled, "Don't push it."

But the ice was broken.

He even stayed for cake, though he complained it was "too sweet—like her dialogue."

Months passed.

The Lighthouse of Despair became a modest success, praised for its humour and "biting self-parody."

Kevin never admitted that he'd meant it seriously.

The Camden Quills returned to their old camaraderie. Arguing about adjectives, laughing at typos, and pretending not to care about sales ranks.

And Kevin, though still allergic to romance, occasionally gave Marianne helpful feedback—like "this metaphor doesn't make me vomit" or "your hero almost has depth now."

Sometimes he even caught himself enjoying her stories.

One evening, after the group disbanded, he lingered behind with Marianne.

"You know," he said grudgingly, "maybe love stories aren't entirely useless."

She smiled. "Careful, Kevin. That sounded like character growth."

He rolled his eyes. "Don't tell anyone. It'll ruin my reputation."

Marianne laughed, packing her notes. "You can't ruin what's already legendary."

Kevin smirked. "True."

They walked out together into the cool Camden night, two writers who'd survived the battlefield of jealousy and emerged, if not friends, then at least fellow travellers in the ridiculous world of storytelling.

As they parted ways, Kevin thought, Maybe there's something to this romance nonsense after all.

Then he shook his head.

"Still," he muttered, "if she puts me in her next book, I'm suing."

My Allergies

How to explain this ocean in my eyes?
a sudden, salty wash I can't command?
It's been five months today since you left.
For me, a lifetime since your soft, familiar hand
smoothed back the hair from my bewildered face.

They see the shine, the pooling at the rim.
The quick, hot spill I try to catch in haste, a trembling
light that makes my vision dim.
"Oh, allergies," I laugh, a sound like gravel.
"The season's brutal, all this pollen dust,"
A lie that's easier for them to unravel than the frayed,
breaking thread of my loss.

They nod, accepting this convenient mask, unaware that
the truth I'm trying to withhold is that the air itself is now a
husk of what it was when you breathed it with me.
It's not the ragweed or the flowering tree.
It's the silence where your morning laughter lay.
The phantom scent of you next to me.

No, these tears are dust from a shattered urn.
The silent echo of your voice as you walk in through the
door.
They are the sounds that I cannot burn of all the love I'll
never give you more.

They are the payment for the dreams we stored.
I say "allergies," my love, but I mean: I miss you so.
And every drop was just a moment ago.

The Beginner's Guide to Accidental Witchcraft

Harold Cartwright wasn't what you'd call "magically inclined."

He was what you'd call "the sort of man who once tried to boil water in a toaster because the kettle looked tired."

So, naturally, when Harold's cousin Denise asked him to help clean out Aunt Myrtle's attic, fate decided this was the perfect moment to introduce him to the occult.

"Just toss anything that looks cursed," Denise had said, waving a hand from the bottom of the stairs. "If it hisses or glows, we don't keep it."

Sound advice thought Harold.

Though he wasn't sure how to recognise a hiss.

Did furniture hiss?

Half an hour later, buried under a pile of porcelain cats and tax receipts from 1973, Harold found a book.

It was thick, bound in cracked leather, and had a faint smell of cinnamon and bad decisions. The cover read: "Grimoire of Moderate Enchantments and Mild Inconveniences."

Harold, being the sort of man who thought "grimoire" was just "grammar" with a typo, assumed it was an old English guide to manners or perhaps soup.

He blew off the dust and opened it.

Instantly, the attic filled with the faint sound of whispering and what might have been a goose sneezing.

The words shimmered and rearranged themselves into neat English.

"Welcome, novice," said the book.

Harold blinked. "Pardon?"

"I said, welcome, novice. You have opened The Grimoire of Moderate Enchantments. Please state your magical name."

Harold coughed. "Er... Harold?"

"Harold," the book repeated, in a voice that sounded vaguely judgmental. "Are you sure?"

"Quite sure, yes."

"Fine," sighed the grimoire. "Harold, it is. What shall we conjure today?"

Now, Harold wasn't stupid.

He knew books weren't meant to talk unless they were being reviewed on the radio. But curiosity (and mild dehydration) got the better of him.

"Something simple," he said. "Perhaps a cup of chamomile tea."

There was a puff of purple smoke, a mild crackling sound, and then, plop, a mug appeared on a nearby trunk. Steam curled from it, fragrant and inviting.

"Oh!" said Harold, delighted. "That's actually." He sipped it. "Chicken soup."

"Close enough," said the grimoire.

"Tea and soup are in the same family of hot liquids. You're welcome."

Over the next hour, Harold experimented.

He asked for a sandwich and got a suspiciously animate loaf that called him "sir."

He requested light and was rewarded with a small sun hovering near his head that complained about "poor working conditions."

And when he tried to summon "a tidy room," every piece of clutter simply vanished into Denise's Toyota parked outside.

The grimoire seemed increasingly cranky.

"Honestly," it said, "you're treating me like an Amazon delivery service."

Harold frowned. "Aren't you supposed to help me do magic?"

"I'm supposed to help qualified witches," the book said. "You, Harold, are about as magical as a damp bagel."

That hurt.

Harold prided himself on being at least a slightly dry bagel.

When Denise finally came up to check on him, Harold was sitting cross-legged on the floor, surrounded by floating spoons, a small thundercloud, and what looked suspiciously like a talking hedgehog in a waistcoat.

"Harold," she drawled, "what have you done?"

"I believe I've achieved sorcery," Harold said proudly.

The hedgehog sneezed sparks. "Technically, it's hedge-magic," it said.

Denise pinched the bridge of her nose. "You found Myrtle's grimoire, didn't you?"

"Yes!" Harold said. "Wonderful book. Bit rude, though."

"Of course it's rude," she muttered. "Aunt Myrtle trapped her ex-boyfriend's soul in it back in the '70s."

The book groaned.

"You told him?! Denise, I thought we agreed never to discuss the incident with the disco pants!"

Denise glared at it. "You deserved it, Clive."

As family revelations go, this one was right up there with "Uncle George used to be in a mime troupe."

"So," Harold said, "the book is... alive?"

"Sentient," corrected the grimoire. "And cursed with impeccable taste."

"Well," Harold said cheerfully, "maybe we can—"

Before he could finish, the floating sun let out a tiny yawn and exploded into confetti.

"Oh, for heaven's sake," the grimoire said. "You've destabilised your aura."

"I've what?"

"Your aura. Your energy field. It's like your Wi-Fi signal, only stickier."

Harold clapped his hands. "Can it be fixed?"

"Possibly," said the book. "If you perform the Ritual of Harmonious Undoing."

"Sounds easy."

"It isn't. It involves interpretive dance."

Ten minutes later, Denise stood at the foot of the attic stairs, listening to her cousin stomp around upstairs to the faint tune of "Stayin' Alive."

"Left foot, spin, arms like a seagull!" barked the grimoire.

"I'm doing it!" Harold yelled.

"Not like that! You look like a confused otter!"

The attic shook.

A puff of glitter burst through the cracks in the ceiling.

Then silence.

Denise climbed the stairs carefully.

The thundercloud was gone.

So were the floating spoons.

The hedgehog sat calmly in a teacup, humming.

Harold was lying flat on the floor, dazed but smiling.

"Did it work?" she asked.

He sat up. "I think so. Everything feels... calmer."

The grimoire coughed politely.

"Yes, yes, all very balanced now. I suppose I should thank you for releasing me from my magical hangover."

"Wonderful," Denise said. "Now close it before—"

But Harold, ever the curious soul, had already turned another page.

It read: "Chapter Two: Summoning Companions for Lonely Evenings."

There was a low hum.

A breeze swept through the attic.

The floorboards glowed faintly.

And suddenly, standing before them, was a woman wearing bell-bottoms, smelling of patchouli, and glaring at the grimoire.

"CLIVE!" she shouted.

The book snapped shut like a guilty child. "Oh, no."

"Aunt Myrtle?" Denise squeaked.

"Indeed!" said the apparition, tossing her hair. "Who dared open my grimoire?"

Harold raised a timid hand. "Er... me. Harold. Big fan."

She looked him up and down.

"You? You're the one who reactivated my spell book with chicken soup?"

"It was an honest mistake," he said.

She sighed. "Mortals."

The book mumbled, "He's not entirely mortal. He dances like a dead fairy."

What followed was, by any standard, an awkward family reunion.

Myrtle, who had apparently transcended death but not drama, declared that Harold was her "magical heir."

Denise tried to argue that Harold once got banned from IKEA in Marsden Park for misusing a fire extinguisher. The grimoire muttered about needing a stiff drink.

But Myrtle was unstoppable.

"You," she said, pointing at Harold, "will continue my work. You will learn the sacred arts. You will respect the grimoire."

Harold nodded meekly. "Of course, Aunt Myrtle."

"And above all," she continued, "you will never use it to make soup again."

"Yes, Aunt Myrtle."

She glowed faintly, satisfied. "Good. Now, as for Clive..."

The book yelped.

"I've changed, Myrtle! I'm a better person now. Well, book."

Myrtle smirked.

"We'll see."

With that, she vanished in a swirl of glitter and faint disco music, leaving behind a faint smell of gin.

Weeks passed.

Harold kept the grimoire in his kitchen cupboard, right between the instant noodles and the sugar.

Occasionally, it offered unsolicited advice.

"Your aura's drooping," it would say.

Or: "You should really stop microwaving eggs."

Once, it even gave him a recipe for lemon biscuits that turned out alarmingly good.

Denise visited one afternoon and found Harold sitting in the garden, the grimoire propped open on a deckchair beside him, both of them wearing sunglasses.

"How's the witchcraft going?" she asked.

"Brilliantly," Harold said. "I've learned how to charm pigeons away from the shed, summon exact change for when I need to pay for a coffee at the Northport Café & Bistro, and—" he leaned in—"make my neighbour's Wi-Fi go faster."

The grimoire preened. "A modest but promising pupil."

Denise eyed the book. "And Myrtle?"

"Still haunting the toaster," said Harold.

"It makes an excellent medium."

Just then, the toaster popped, and Myrtle's voice drifted out faintly: "Don't burn the bread, Harold!"

Denise sighed. "You know, most people just get Alexa."

Harold shrugged.

"Alexa doesn't bake biscuits or lecture me about aura stability."

The grimoire chuckled.

"Nor does she appreciate good company."

Harold grinned.

"True. Besides, every wizard needs a talking book."

"I'm not just a talking book," the grimoire said. "I'm a lifestyle choice."

And that's how Harold Cartwright, part-time handyperson and full-time hazard, became Northport's only certified "Domestic Warlock."

His spells remained modest, like finding lost socks or slightly improving takeaway pizza, but he was happy.

Because every evening, as the sun dipped and the world grew quiet, he'd sit with his tea (or soup) and his snarky, enchanted grimoire, grateful that some accidents, especially magical ones, turned out rather well.

"Ready for another spell, Harold?" the grimoire would ask.

"Only if it doesn't involve dancing."

"No promises."

And somewhere faintly from the toaster:

"Left foot, spin, arms like a seagull!"

Echoes of You

I wake in a quiet bedroom where your laughter used to blossom
Your picture by the nightstand makes the silence loom
With every sound from the radio, I hear your name
As I walk around our home, I feel the weight of this pain

Your favourite jumper hangs in the closet
I still catch your scent drifting through the air
As I look out the patio and speak to the moon, hoping you'll reply
But at night, the silent stars answer with a sigh

I'll try to hold on to every moment we had
I'll try to reach for our love, but it remains beyond
I know we will meet again somewhere above
Until then, I'll carry you within me, my undying love

You were my everything, my muse to my words
Now I'm chasing shadows of us as I reach for your heart
Though the world moves on, I'll stay where I am
Until you call me to be by your side

The Grabatologist Guide to Disaster*

My name is Martin Clutch, and I am a grabatologist — a professional collector and analyst of ties.

Yes, neckties.

The long, silky nooses of modern civilization.

Don't laugh; this is a real field of study.

The Australian Society of Grabatology even sent me a certificate. I printed it myself, but it still counts.

You might wonder how one becomes a grabatologist.

It all began in 1987, when my uncle Gerald left me his entire collection of novelty ties upon his death, all 412 pieces ranging from a glow-in-the-dark "Moon Landing" to a woollen monstrosity that depicted Santa surfing on a reindeer.

When I wore one to a job interview at a bank, the manager said, "That tie is an abomination."

I didn't get the job, but I got something far more valuable: a calling.

Since then, I've made it my mission to study, catalogue, and preserve ties as humanity's last form of wearable art — and sometimes accidental weaponry (ask me about the "rotating piano key" incident of 2003).

My week began splendidly. The International Grabatologists' Conference (IGC) was coming up, and this year it was being held at the Pelican Pub in the Sydney CBD, where all the world's leading tie experts, all six of us, would gather.

I was scheduled to present my magnum opus: "The Semiotics of Polyester Ducks: A Postmodern Reinterpretation."

I had the perfect tie for the occasion.

A rare 1970s "Mallard in Flight" print, silk, with only minor gravy stains (from my experimental "tie lunch napkin" phase). Unfortunately, my cat, Lady Windsor, had chosen that tie as her latest victim. I found her curled up on it like Cleopatra on a sofa.

"Lady Windsor," I hissed, "you have no appreciation for historical textiles."

She yawned.

Desperate, I attempted to iron the wrinkles out. Note to self: do not use the "cotton + steam + rage" setting. The ducks warped. They looked like melting Salvador Dalí birds.

I'd have to improvise.

My neighbour, Mrs Button, runs a thrift shop full of what she calls "pre-loved" clothing.

I call it "pre-sweated."

Still, she sometimes gets rare ties in stock.

So, I put on my best "collector's expression" a mix of authority and mild superiority and strode in.

"Morning, Martin," she said, squinting at me. "Still studying strings for the neck?"

"Mrs Button," I said, "I'm advancing human understanding of symbolic attire. We are the only species to willingly knot fabric around our windpipes."

She grunted. "There's a bin of ties by the toilet. Help yourself."

And that's where I found it: the Holy Grail of Neckties.

A 1964 Beatles tie featuring cartoon versions of the Fab Four.

My heart skipped. My palms sweated.

My glasses fogged.

I whispered, "Hello, gorgeous. Come to Daddy," like a man in a perfume commercial.

"Five dollars," Mrs Button said.

I reached for my wallet, but a rival grabatologist, Professor Dennis Blight, appeared like a tie-wielding Dracula.

"Martin," he sneered, "still collecting novelty tat, are we?"

"Dennis," I said sweetly, "still confusing novelty with heritage?"

He lunged for the Beatles' tie.

I lunged too.

We collided, toppling into a rack of cardigans. Buttons rained down like shrapnel. When the dust settled, Mrs Button was holding the tie.

"You two fight over this thing like seagulls over a chip," she snapped. "It's mine until you both leave."

We both left, I in disgrace, Dennis in smug triumph, and the tie still hanging behind her counter. I plotted revenge that night while polishing my "Mathematical Equations" tie (featuring equations I still don't understand).

The next morning, I found Dennis on Facebook boasting about his "new acquisition." He even posted a photo of himself wearing my Beatles tie — crooked, no less.

I exposed him for the fraud he was.

You see, Dennis has a secret: he wears clip-ons.

A true grabatologist considers clip-ons heresy, like instant coffee or AI poetry. At the conference, I would unveil photographic proof of Dennis Blight, the Clip-On Conman.

My assistant (that is, my niece Emily, who helps in exchange for "not being mentioned online") agreed to help me capture the evidence. I instructed her to infiltrate Dennis's hotel suite with a camera. She pointed out that this was both illegal and creepy. I told her it was for science.

She sighed. "You're lucky you're my weird uncle."

The IGC began with the usual chaos.

Someone spilled coffee on a display of 1930s bow ties; another delegate tried to argue that bolo ties counted (they don't), and a man from Prague showed how to tie a Windsor knot using only his feet.

My presentation was scheduled after lunch, a bad slot.

Everyone would be sleepy and digesting conference chicken.

But I had an edge: scandal.

As I set up my PowerPoint — "Ties Through the Ages: From Cravat to Catastrophe" — I saw Dennis preening in the front row, Beatles tie gleaming.

"Ladies and gentlemen," I began, "today I will explore not only the aesthetics of neckwear but also the ethics."

Dramatic pause.

"For what is a tie if not a symbol of truth, of integrity, of honesty?"

A murmur ran through the crowd. Dennis shifted in his seat.

"That," I said, pointing to the screen, "is a man who betrays our noble craft."

Click. Emily's photo appeared: Dennis in his hotel room mirror, wearing a clip-on tie.

Gasps erupted. Someone screamed. The moderator fainted.

Dennis leapt up. "That's Photoshop!"

"Oh, really?" I asserted. "Care to remove your tie and prove it?"

He hesitated.

Then, trembling, he tugged.

The tie snapped off.

The room fell silent except for the gentle hiss of the projector fan.

It was glorious.

Until, of course, the tie — being a vintage clip-on — ricocheted through the air and smacked the president of the IGC squarely in the forehead.

They banned both of us.

Dennis for "unsanctioned use of weaponized accessories," and me for "public humiliation via PowerPoint."

But I didn't care.

I had restored honour to grabatology.

On the train home, I smiled proudly until I realised Lady Windsor had somehow gotten into my suitcase and was now sleeping on my emergency backup tie, the "Solar System" print.

I sighed. "You're a menace, Windsor."

She purred, rolled over, and revealed she'd coughed up a hairball in the middle of Saturn's rings.

These days, I continue my work from home, cataloguing new acquisitions on my website "TiesThatBind.com."

I give lectures to small audiences (mainly my cat and occasionally my neighbour's parrot), and I've started writing a book: Fifty Shades of Grey Silk: A Grabatologist's Memoir.

People often ask me why I devote my life to neckties, and I tell them: because ties are humanity's most ridiculous invention.

They serve no purpose; they choke us slightly, and yet men wear them proudly. They're proof that civilization isn't logical.

It's fashionable.

So yes, I may be a grabatologist, but I'm also a philosopher.

One with an extensive wardrobe and several mild burn scars from ironing accidents.

And if you ever meet me in person, don't laugh at my tie.

Because I assure you — it's studying you, too.

*Dear reader, my late wife told me when I first moved to Sydney that Australians called garbage collectors 'garbologists,' and of course I laughed, thinking she was pulling my leg, but that was not the case. I came to determine that Australia uses the term "garbologist" (and related "garbo") to humorously yet respectfully describe refuse collectors and to refer to the study of waste to understand human behaviour and improve recycling. Stemming from the 1960s, it blends "garbage" with "-ologist" to define specialists in analysing household and commercial refuse.

The Ripples We Leave Behind

The ducks arrive before I do. They always have. Each morning, as the sun lifts itself reluctantly above the gum trees, I walk the narrow path that leads to the pond.

It's close to the house — our house — though it feels further now, as if grief stretches distance the way heat bends air.

I stand where I always stand, just at the edge, hands at my side.

"Another cold winter," I mumbled to myself as I exhaled and saw my breath as it formed a faint mist in the cool air, and the pond mirrored it back — calm, silver, and half-asleep.

Then, the ducks start their dance.

One lands with a soft splash, followed by another, and another, until the water trembles in widening circles. Ripples intersect and fade, tiny signatures of movement that vanish almost as soon as they begin. I watch them until my eyes blur, and I can no longer tell where one wave ends, and another begins.

That's when I talk to her.

"You'd laugh," I whisper. "They still argue over who gets the best landing spot."

I smile because I can almost hear her reply — that half-teasing, half-tender tone she used whenever I pointed out something obvious. 'They're ducks, love. They're meant to argue.' The silence that follows is thick. Heavy. Beautiful in its way.

It's been a year since she passed, and yet I still catch myself walking in step with her ghost. She used to say the pond was our little cathedral — that nature, not brick or stained glass, was where God hid best.

We used to stand here in quiet reverence, her hand looped through my arm, listening to the wind move through the reeds like whispered hymns.

Now, it's only me.

I see the ducks skim the surface again, their wings beating, their feet slapping the water in a flash of motion that feels both chaotic and sacred, and yet beautiful.

As they lift off, the light slices through the mist, and some droplets sparkle like cosmic dust. For an instant, it all looked to me as if it was a painting, like a frame from an old movie, too vivid to be real.

It's in those moments, when light and memory collide, that I feel her most.

As though she's woven into the shimmer like a part of the morning itself.

Sometimes I wonder if the pond remembers her.

She had a habit of tossing tiny leaves, watching the small ripples spread until they stopped. "That's what love does," she once said. "It keeps moving, even when you can't see where it goes."

I hadn't understood it then. I do now. Because grief too ripples.

It moves through everything — my coffee cup, the sound of her favourite song on the radio, the scent of her perfume still faint in the bedroom closet. It changes shape but never truly disappears.

This morning, the sky shifted from pink to gold.

The light catches the thin film of water, and I see both my reflection and hers.

Not the face I knew, not exactly, but something softer, threaded through the light, the way a reflection lingers even after the wind stirs.

"I miss you," I say simply.

The words fall, and the pond carries them outward.

Several ducks circle overhead, their wings catching the sun. I raise my hand, not to wave but to steady myself against the ache that rises suddenly, sharply.

The world goes still for a heartbeat: air, water, grief, and in that stillness, I swear I hear her voice again.

"Keep walking, love."

So, I do.

I take a slow step, then another, the footpath filled with leaves crunching beneath my runners. The sound anchors me to the earth. Around me, life moves.

Ducks land, ripples spread, the wind stirs.

Everything begins again, as it must.

And as I turn toward home, the pond behind me shimmers with impossible clarity, as if some unseen hand had wiped the world clean.

I don't look back. I don't have to.

Because love, like ripples, is never really gone.

It just keeps moving outward until it becomes part of everything.

Things to Keep

I am not a saint. I say this first, so you don't mistake my quiet for virtue, or my small routines for goodness. I work at the lost property desk at Central Station, which sounds like a penance people make up for characters in stories—lonely men tending to other people's missing things. But I took the job because the hours suited my life and because most things do not ask to be forgiven; they just sit and wait until someone remembers them.

Between the morning rush and the evening rush, there is a hush that settles over the station like a cool sheet. I log items into the registry: a blue scarf smelling faintly of cardamom, a cracked phone with a photo of a spaniel as the wallpaper, a left shoe, a wedding program, a plastic dinosaur with one eye rubbed off. I give each a number, a brief description, and a date. Names rarely enter it. People lose the object first and the meaning later. It goes that way with people too.

The rules are simple. Don't rifle pockets. Don't judge a life crammed inside a bag. Don't keep what doesn't belong to you. I have kept things, though—only one, really, and not because I needed it. Because I wanted something of hers, and wanting is the opposite of sainthood.

She came on a wet Thursday. I remember because the ceiling lights cast halos on the tiles and everyone moved quickly, heads down, the station smelling of wool and rain. She had a yellow umbrella, the exact yellow of lemon rind, and a laugh that slipped out when she shook water from it and drenched her own shoes. She apologised to them. Then she turned to me and said, "I think I lost my notebook on the train from Kogarah. Spiral-bound, red cover, looks like a schoolbook. Has a sticker of a whale on it."

"Whale sticker," I said, writing. "Red, spiral, schoolish." I smiled. You learn to reflect people's moods at this desk, a cheap way to make them feel seen. "If it comes in, I'll tag it with 'pod.'"

She laughed at that and leaned in to read my scrawl. She smelled of something citrus and cool. "Do you actually tag things with jokes?"

"Only when the day needs saving." I kept the tone easy and professional. The ring on her finger was thin and silver. No stone. Could be anything.

She tapped the counter with her knuckles. "I'm a teacher," she said, as though it explained everything. "Half of my brain is in that notebook."

"Teachers are our most frequent return customers," I said. "Right after toddlers."

"Toddlers come here?"

"By proxy. Teddies, mostly."

She grinned, checked her watch, and left me her number. "If it turns up, will you call? Even late."

"It usually takes a day," I said. "People return things after they remember having a conscience."

"I'll take my chances," she said, and raised her umbrella like a toast before vanishing into the press of commuters.

I found the notebook three hours later, wedged under a bench on Platform 18. I tell myself that if I'd found it earlier, nothing would have changed; time is not a thread you can simply pull. Still, I took the long way back because the sky had scoured itself to a thin blue and the pigeons were doing their bumbling courtships, and because the longer I carried the notebook, the more precious it felt, warm from my arm.

The red cover had the whale sticker, smiling a grin too wide. Inside, her handwriting marched in tidy lines: lesson plans, lists, names of songs she wanted to learn on the guitar. Pages of small sketches—a gum tree, a mug with steam, a cat with a sullen glare. Then, there was a page titled simply, "Things to Keep." There were only four items: "honesty," "the old kettle," "the way Mum said my name," and "Saturday mornings."

I closed it and felt—what? Envy, maybe, for the certainty of keeping. I set it on my desk, logged it as 'Found. Red notebook. Whale sticker.' I stared at the phone number she'd left.

I did not call. If you're looking for a reason, you can choose any: professional boundaries, the late hour, the hope she'd come in herself. Pick one that makes me better than I was. The truth is that I liked the idea of her walking toward me through the station's long corridor more than the ordinary ring of a phone. I wanted the world to deliver her, not a wire.

The next day, she didn't come. Nor the next. On Monday, a man in a navy jacket came instead. He had the posture of someone who had rehearsed being calm. He asked for a red notebook with a whale sticker.

"She left her number," I said, and something in his face flinched at the pronoun.

"I'm her husband," he said, and the word made a space around itself like a dropped spoon in a quiet room. He passed me a driver's license with her name and his address and waited. "She was struck crossing Princes Highway on Friday night," he said. "They took her to St George. She died that evening. I found a note on our fridge about the notebook." He managed a smile that had nothing to do with happiness. "She always left herself notes. I thought, if she was going to worry about it, I should make sure it got back to her."

I handed him the notebook. "I'm so sorry." The phrase felt like a postcard you send because one must. I wanted to tell him she had laughed, and the exact shape of it, and that she had apologised to her shoes. She loved Saturday mornings. But these were not mine to give.

He nodded and took it with both hands. "Thank you," he said, and left carefully, as if the air had sharp corners.

For a long time afterward, the station felt different. The light too white, the floor too clean, everything containing the outline of what wasn't there. I did the work because work is what you do when words fail. I logged umbrellas and bags, a violin in a foam case, a ring in a dishcloth. When the ring's owner phoned to describe it, I put a note on the entry: "Cried with relief. Husband deployed. Gift from Mum." The registry became a book of small human weather reports. I started adding the details I'd previously resisted: a sticker, a smell, a sigh. It didn't break the rules. It just felt like holding something carefully.

At night, I walked past the café where she might have sat on a Saturday morning. It wasn't grief in the usual sense. I had divorced quietly five years ago; the marriage fading like a banner left in the sun. My son speaks to me on Sundays because calendars are persuasive. What I felt was the particular ache of unrealised conversation, of a life that brushed yours as lightly as a sleeve and then was gone. A missingness that didn't belong to me and still settled inside me like a tenant.

Months went by. The trains kept their old promises—arrive, depart, arrive, depart. I grew a habit of looking for yellow. I wanted to see umbrellas, lemons, the edge of a raincoat. I wanted to look and be mistaken.

In spring, a woman came with a little girl whose hair had been braided with too much determination. The girl clutched a soft whale. The woman's face had a hopefulness that frightened me, a way of scanning the room as if it might produce what she needed through politeness alone.

"We lost a ring," she said. "Gold, thin, with no stone. It's my sister's." She slid a paper across the counter: the description written in a careful hand, the address, a name. Not the same name, but I heard it anyway: the lilting way Mum said my name. I checked the registry. "Found in May," I said. "No one claimed it. We hold for ninety days before we..." I stopped. Sometimes the procedure sounds like a threat.

She waited. The girl's whale stared from the counter, grinning.

I brought out the plastic tray of unclaimed rings. The woman sifted delicately, as if selecting words to say at a bedside. She found it quickly, her breath catching. "This one," she said, and the relief that came off her felt almost visible, a heat shimmer. "It was my sister's wedding ring. She died last year. We kept meaning to switch it to a chain, but grief rearranges your furniture."

I nodded. She offered to pay. I said no. She asked how to thank me. I said she just had.

After they left, I took my logbook and wrote for the ring: "Returned to sister. Kept grief from hardening."

I understood that what I could do was small, and also not small. I couldn't call the dead back. But I could hand over a warm scarf to someone shivering at the edges. I could say, "Yes, it's here," and for a moment in a vast, rattling world, make the space around a person soften.

A year passed. I bought a kettle like the old kind, the sort that whistles, because the hiss and rise of its sound felt like a promise kept to no one in particular. On Saturdays, I tried to sit somewhere, the way she had written. I ordered toast and marmalade. I read the paper. Sometimes I brought a notebook and wrote lists: songs I heard on the radio, names of trees, the odd joke I'd like to remember. I put "honesty" at the top of each page, as a dare.

I am not a saint. I kept the thin scrap of paper where she had written her number. It sits in my wallet behind my bus pass, softened by time and receipt lint. I take it out occasionally and imagine calling. I don't, not because of boundaries, but because the number belongs to a Thursday where rain ran off the station roof and a woman lifted a yellow umbrella like a toast. I don't want to speak into the silence that comes after that. I want the silence to do as silence does: make room.

Some days, a man in a navy jacket passes through the concourse. He has the face of every husband and none. I think of stepping out to him and saying what I didn't: that the last thing his wife cared about retrieving, on the day the world ended for her, was a notebook full of small, careful things. That she left behind a page titled "Things to Keep," and that he is likely written there somewhere invisible, under all of it. That strangers remember her briefly, like a sun-warmed railing you touch and then let go.

I don't step out. I log what is found. I answer the phone. I keep the kettle on the little hot plate under the desk and pour into a paper cup. The station quiets and fills, quiets, and fills. The loudspeaker tells us what is coming, not what has passed.

If redemption exists for men like me, it looks like this: a desk, a ledger, a careful hand. A voice that says, "Yes, I have it," and another that says, "Thank you," and in between, an ordinary exchange that staves off the feeling we are irretrievably scattered. You can call that a routine if you want. You can say it is not sainthood. I will not argue.

But I have learned that almost nothing is truly lost. It waits—sometimes for hours, sometimes for years—for someone to recognise it and say its name. And when they do, I get to see the world, for a second, stitched back together, not by miracles, but by returning.

The Closer of Worlds

Elara was a conservator, not an executioner. This was the mantra she whispered a thousand times per cycle as the worlds dimmed around her.

She destroyed nothing.

She stabilised the collapse, ensuring that the essence—the cumulative memory, the unique vibrational frequency, the ghost of every laughter and tear—didn't simply dissipate into the cold, chaotic static of the Void.

Her title, The Closer of Worlds, was earned with the gravitas of a necessary sorrow.

Her current task was Kaelen, the third world in her quadrant this year.

It was a water-world, a sphere of deep sapphire and emerald islands, but its orbit was decaying. The gravity of its twin sons, once a harmonious dance, had become a tightening embrace, promising tidal waves that would swallow mountains.

Physics doomed the world, and Elara was here to manage the inevitable.

She stood on the highest spire of the floating capital, a crystalline structure built by the long-vanished Makers.

Beneath her, the ocean glittered under the bruised, sunset-coloured sky.

The inhabitants, the Kaela, were already gone.

Millennia ago, they had mastered light travel, leaving behind only structures and ghosts of light.

She was collecting the echoes.

In her hands, she held the Archive, a dense, smooth sphere of obsidian that pulsed with a faint, warm light—the collective repository of every world she had ever closed.

It was a crushing weight, heavier than any metal, yet she carried it without effort. It held the knowledge of ten thousand realities, and with Kaelen, it would hold ten thousand and one.

She activated the first resonance sequence.

A low, powerful hum vibrated through the spire, not a sound heard by the ear, but felt in the bone.

It was the universe sighing.

This frequency sought the residual consciousness—the environmental memory that clung to every drop of water, every grain of sand, every pane of glass.

"Don't fight the pull," she thought, projecting the message through the spire and across the trembling oceans. "It is safe now. It is time to rest."

As the Archive absorbed the essence, phantom images flickered around her.

A Kaela child, laughing as a tiny aquatic drone zipped through the air.

An elderly scholar traced the patterns of the waves with a wrinkled finger.

A silent moment between two lovers under the pale double moons.

They were just data now, fleeting projections of stored energy, but they hurt Elara with a profound, aching beauty.

Her eyes, usually cold and steady, welled up.

Each world felt like a volume in a library being carefully shelved, not burned. But closing a world still meant erasing it from the present tense, moving it into the irreversible past.

She was the one who turned the key.

The hardest part was always the last anchor point—the place where the world's self-awareness was strongest.

For Kaelen, it was a single, ancient stone at the base of the spire, engraved with the first words the Kaela ever wrote: We are the light that finds the water.

Elara knelt, placing one hand on the stone and the other on the Archive.

The Archive flared, drinking the final, deep-blue pulse of Kaelen's collective soul.

The phantom images dissolved.

The humming stopped.

Silence.

Not the silence of peace, but the echoing, absolute, crushing silence of an empty cathedral.

Kaelen was now a dead planet, an inert mass spiralling toward its fate.

Its memory was safe, a new thread woven into the fabric of the Archive, ready to be reintegrated into the next, nascent universe when the great Cycle turned.

Elara stood, the obsidian sphere feeling marginally heavier. She looked out at the Dead Sea; her silhouette framed against the impending astronomical disaster.

She was ten thousand and one worlds old.

For her, time was measured not in years, but in the rise and fall of civilisations. She remembered the fire-worlds, the ice-worlds, the worlds made entirely of crystal song, and the worlds, like Kaelen, which were simply beautiful.

She turned from the spire, pulling a ripple in the fabric of space-time, and stepped back into the infinite, non-existent space she called home.

It was a grey, featureless expanse, containing only herself and the Archive.

The voice, which was really just her own echoing mind, spoke.

"Cycle count: 10,001. Mission successful. Closer."

Elara didn't respond.

She never did.

She just stood there, waiting for the universe to begin its slow, violent process of creating the next world, the next brief, flickering candle she would inevitably be asked to extinguish, to conserve, and to carry.

Her sorrow was the price of existence, and she paid it, world after world, cycle after cycle.

She was The Closer, and her work was never truly done.

The Librarian's Curse

The Northport Public Library on a quiet Tuesday afternoon was a sanctuary of hushed intentions and deferred responsibilities.

It was a place where the loudest sound was the aggressive shush of a dedicated patron or the almost subsonic hum of air conditioning fighting literary dust mites.

But for Elias Thorne, things were anything but quiet. Elias was the protagonist, if you could call him that, of a volume titled The Calculus of Consequence: A Meditative Study of 18th-Century Belgian Tax Law.

At 412 pages in, he stood eternally by a foggy, lead-paned window of a fictional Brussels manor, lamenting the inevitable decay of the industrial spirit. His world was monochrome, his waistcoat was scratchy, and his internal monologue was 90% despair and 10% deeply researched melancholy about tariffs on hops.

"Alas," he muttered, adjusting a fictional cravat of profound disappointment. "The weight of history is an anvil upon the soul, and the future is but a poorly drafted ledger."

This afternoon, Elias's book had been abandoned face-up on a mahogany reading table, precisely three inches away from another, significantly brighter volume.

Stellar Bake-Off: My Disaster Date with the Astronaut's Brother.

The protagonist of this volume, Roxana "Roxy" Bloom, was mid-catastrophe on page 78, standing amidst what looked like a glitter-bomb explosion of failed meringue in a brightly lit, implausibly chic Brooklyn kitchen.

Her world smelled strongly of burnt sugar, her sneakers were hot pink, and her internal monologue was 90% caffeine and 10% highly judgmental observations about men who described their jobs as "disrupting the artisanal bagel space."

"Seriously, Chelsea," Roxy was currently exclaiming to her best friend (who was, tragically, on the adjacent page and couldn't see the existential crisis unfolding three inches away), "I told him I was a competitive baker, not a historical re-enactor. I swear, if he uses the phrase 'curate my feelings' one more time, I'm going to use his artisanal sourdough starter as a weapon."

Suddenly, the air between the pages shimmered. It wasn't the heat of the library or a sudden shift in the narrative.

It was a contact.

Elias's theatrical sigh, a deep, chest-rattling rumination on the economic fallout of the Napoleonic Wars, was so profound it caused the paper in the opposite book, Roxy's, to flutter.

Roxy, whose attention was highly distractible, looked up from her reflection in the stainless-steel mixing bowl.

"Did that meringue just breathe?" she whispered, scanning the edges of the text block.

"A thousand pardons, Madame," came a low, velvety voice that smelled distinctly of antique leather and old tea.

Elias, whose peripheral vision was excellent for detecting looming historical precedent, had finally noticed the sudden, alarming flash of pink and neon green across the chasm of the book gutter.

"My apologies. My melancholy is occasionally... texturally intrusive."

Roxy blinked, and she took in the sight of him: a man in full period dress, looking absolutely gutted about a ledger, framed by a title page featuring the smallest, most depressing lithograph of a tax stamp she had ever seen.

"Melancholy is texturally intrusive?" She scoffed, placing her hands on her hips. "Honey, you look like you just got stood up by a very depressing funeral. Who are you, and why does your ambiance feel like a filter set to 'Victorian Plague'?"

Elias was staggered.

Never had a fictional construct addressed him with such vibrant, unforgiving bluntness. His usual conversational partners were deceased philosophers or a stoic manservant named Grimsby, who communicated only via eyebrow arches.

"I am Elias Thorne, Doctor of Jurisprudence and chronicler of the inevitable descent of the human condition into administrative oversight," he declared, attempting to bow across the spine of the book. "And I perceive you are an entity saturated in primary colours, inhabiting a world seemingly devoid of proper historical context."

Roxy crossed her arms.

"Roxana Bloom, world-class baker, currently dealing with the fallout of dating a man who thinks 'gluten-free' is a personality trait. And, uh, 'devoid of historical context' is kind of the point. My book has a happy ending. Yours sounds like it has an index and a bibliography."

Elias sighed again, a sound that threatened to crease Page 413.

"A happy ending? A ludicrous fictional invention. My fate is to be analysed by weary college students and occasionally used as a doorstop. What is your narrative arc if I may ask?"

"My arc," Roxy stated, gesturing around her kitchen, "is to win a baking competition, realise the true meaning of friendship, and probably kiss a cute guy who isn't pretentious. Right now, I'm trying to figure out how to transport fifty mini-cheesecakes to the finals without them melting. What's your current plot point?"

"I am struggling with the inherent moral ambiguity of the 1795 excise tax on imported French brandy," Elias replied solemnly.

There was a moment of silence.

"Wow," Roxy said. "That's the saddest thing I have ever heard, and I once baked a cake shaped like a breakup letter."

She leaned in, her brightly drawn face inches from the gutter.

"Look, Elias. You need to lighten up. My world has sunlight and coffee that doesn't taste like boiled despair. Your world has great jackets, but zero fun."

Elias felt a pull, a curiosity that transcended the carefully researched gloom of his text. Her proximity was an electric, chaotic shock. His world felt heavier, more textured, when contrasted with her effervescent presence.

"Miss Bloom," he murmured, dropping the 'Doctor of Jurisprudence,' pretence. "Your luminosity is quite disarming. It is an unexpected pleasure to find such a vibrant spirit dwelling so near to my chapter on punitive governmental levies."

"It's Roxy," she corrected, softening her tone.

She felt sorry for him, trapped in a leather-bound tomb.

"And you're kind of adorable when you're not talking about taxation. For a guy stuck in a perpetual rainstorm, you're surprisingly well-adjusted."

"Well-adjusted is merely a temporary reprieve from existential dread, Roxy," Elias said, a faint, almost dangerous smile playing on his lips.

He was enjoying this transgression.

Flirting with a woman from a rom-com felt like breaking every single 18th-century law simultaneously.

"I feel, dare I say it, a spark. A fleeting, rebellious warmth against the cold logic of fate."

"A spark!" Roxy giggled. "See? You're learning! Okay, Elias Thorne, Dr. Doom. Tell me your deepest desire. Right now. Quick, before a character walks onto your page and asks you about the yield curve."

Elias took a metaphorical deep breath of his dusty manor air.

"I wish, well, I wish simply to feel the sun, not merely to contemplate its philosophical meaning. And perhaps, just perhaps, to witness a dessert that does not carry the weight of socio-economic failure."

"Done," Roxy said instantly. "My deepest desire is to teach you the difference between a wonderful date and a disastrous one. A date must involve laughter and zero discussion of historical macroeconomics. Say you'll join me, Elias. We'll rewrite your ending."

"I accept your terms, Roxana Bloom," Elias said, his voice husky.

He was ready to jettison three entire chapters on municipal budgeting just to continue this conversation.

"This meeting is the most exhilarating thing to happen in my book since the Great Pig Iron Scandal of 1803."

"Pig Iron Scandal? You guys are so extra. Okay, listen, for our first date, let's talk about—oh, wait."

Roxy's cheerful expression suddenly froze. She felt a strange, pervasive drop in the ambient lighting, a shift in the air pressure that felt less like plot development and more like judgment.

Elias, whose senses were attuned to the subtle vibrations of authority (a useful skill for an 18th-century historian dodging arbitrary laws), felt it, too. A shadow, silent and inescapable, fell across the library table, eclipsing the light that flowed between its pages.

It was Miss Higgins, the head librarian.

Miss Higgins did not walk; she glided, propelled by a dedication to silence and order that bordered on the divine. She wore soft-soled shoes, but they sounded like the marching of destiny.

She was the one true villain on the Northport shelves: The Closer of Worlds.

Elias instinctively stiffened, trying to melt back into his window frame, hoping the complex syntax of his lamentations would render him invisible.

"Books," Miss Higgins whispered, the sound a dry, rustling hiss that was louder than a shout. "Are to be placed back correctly."

Her hand, massive and pale like a piece of unused parchment, hovered over the two open volumes.

"Oh, no, wait!" Roxy cried, attempting to duck behind a freshly baked lemon tart on her page. "We were just getting to the first kiss! Elias, quick! Say something profound and memorable!"

"The fundamental truth of human existence is our inevitable separation by the cold, unyielding hand of bureaucratic—" Elias began dramatically.

SMACK!

The sound of The Calculus of Consequence closing was final and catastrophic. The light in Elias's world vanished, replaced by the profound, stifling darkness of the endpapers.

"NOOOO!" Roxy screamed, but the thick, glossy cover of Stellar Bake-Off was already descending.

THWUMP!

Miss Higgins sighed, a sound of deep, institutional satisfaction. She picked up the two books.

Elias was racked with existential angst; his internal world was currently a whirlwind of darkness, regret, and the ghost of a neon-pink sneaker.

He was now on Page 413, trapped in the unforgiving void between his last despairing sentence and the first paragraph of a chapter about the French grain shortage.

Roxy was in a similar panic; her world having gone from a bright catastrophe to total blackness.

"He was going to kiss me!" she mentally shrieked to her absent best friend.

"I was going to save him from taxation! This is a plot device I hate!"

Miss Higgins placed Stellar Bake-Off with a silent, precise movement onto the Young Adult shelf. Then, she walked five metres to the opposite end of the library, the Historical Studies Aisle, and slotted The Calculus of Consequence back into its dark, predictable slot.

They were separated.

It seemed kilometres apart, yet only a few steps away.

Elias stood again at his window, adjusting his cravat, but now the fog seemed less profound, more like a temporary annoyance. He muttered his line about the anvil upon the soul, but in his mind, he smelled faint notes of vanilla and burnt meringue, and he wondered, briefly, what a 'disrupting the artisanal bagel space' person looked like.

Roxy, back on page 78, looked forlornly at her lemon tart. The memory of Elias's overly serious, handsome face and his deeply tragic voice had permanently altered her narrative. She thought, Maybe historical re-enactors aren't so bad. At least they know how to wear a good jacket.

The world of The Calculus of Consequence remained bleak, but somewhere on the margin of Page 414, Elias Thorne had drawn a tiny, historically inaccurate heart.

The Secret

The hot summer day had a languid, sleepy quality to it. The air hung thick and shimmering, tasting faintly of baked asphalt and cut grass. It was a heat that turned sound into slow, syrupy motion: the distant, lazy buzz of a lawnmower, the high whine of a cicada that seemed to operate on an eternal loop, the occasional clink of the ice machine next door. I was sprawled on the worn, overstuffed sofa in the living room, ostensibly reading a novel, but mostly tracking the slow, agonizing journey of a single dust motes dancing in the beam of sun slicing through the blinds.

Everything felt coated in a fine, warm film. Even my thoughts were moving slowly, like boats stuck in treacle. I'd been home from college for three weeks, and the initial bliss of freedom had long curdled into a heavy, directional boredom. There was nothing immediate to do, nowhere immediate to go, and the simple act of standing up felt like signing up for an Olympic event.

But eventually, the stillness became too much. The lack of intention felt aggressive. I threw the book onto the floor with a soft thump—a sound that seemed obscenely loud in the quiet house—and pushed myself upright. My shirt immediately clung to my back. I needed a distraction, preferably one that involved things that weren't melting.

I drifted into the back hallway, where the temperature dropped slightly, smelling of old plaster and lemon polish. My destination was the guest room, which hadn't been genuinely used since my great-aunt Beatrice passed away a decade ago. It was a repository of forgotten things, mostly old blankets, and boxed-up holiday décor, but I remembered a large, squat cedar chest in the corner, and I had a sudden, arbitrary urge to see what was inside.

The room was dim, with the curtains drawn against the sun. The air was cool and close, trapped. The cedar chest sat against the far wall, dark wood polished smooth by years of accidental knocks and duster strokes. I knelt down, ignoring the squeak of my jeans, and laid a hand on the cool lid. It smelled exactly like old memories—a deep, musty, woody scent mixed faintly with the lingering sweetness of lavender sachets my mother used to tuck inside.

The clasp was not locked, just stiff. I worked it open, and the heavy lid lifted with a long, drawn-out groan of aged hinges. The smell that billowed out was rich and overpowering: cedar, wool, and the distinct, cloying tang of mothballs. Inside were stacks of quilts, linen tablecloths yellowed by time, and a few crocheted throws I vaguely remembered from my childhood.

I started digging, pulling out heavy items, and piling them onto the cool tile floor. It was mindless work, just what I needed. Halfway down, beneath a thick, scratchy horse's blanket—why did we own a horse blanket?—my fingers brushed against something hard and unyielding. It wasn't fabric. I pulled out a small, boxy container, about the size of a jewellery box, made of dark, unvarnished pine. It wasn't locked, just secured with a small brass hook and loop.

I opened it. Inside, nestled on a bed of slightly disintegrated purple velvet, were two items. The first was a faded photograph, black and white, slightly curling at the edges. It showed two young people in their early twenties sitting in a convertible—the kind with fins, probably from the 1950s. They were laughing uproariously, heads tilted back, their joy so vivid it felt like a sudden gust of cool air in the stuffy room. The man had my grandfather's cheekbones, but younger and looser. The woman... I didn't recognise her. She had startlingly bright eyes and a riot of dark, curly hair.

The second item was a single folded piece of paper—thick, cream-coloured, like expensive stationery. It wasn't a letter; it was just a small note, written in elegant, purposeful cursive that dipped and swirled across the page. It was my grandfather's handwriting.

I unfolded it carefully, my heart doing a quiet, nervous drumroll. The paper was so old I was afraid it would tear.

The note read simply: "You are the best promise I ever made to myself. Please don't forget that." And beneath it, a date: July 12, 1957.

July 12th was my grandmother's birthday. But the woman in the picture wasn't my grandmother.

The sleepy, languid quality of the day shattered instantly. The heat was still there, pressing in, but I didn't feel the boredom anymore. I felt an electric, sharp realisation that the people who raised us, the pillars of our stability, were not always those things. They were once young, reckless, and capable of entire hidden histories that had played out under the very roof I was standing beneath.

I stared at the photograph again, the strange woman's bright, laughing eyes meeting mine across sixty years. What promise had he made? And why did this fragment of their past live here, tucked away in the darkest corner of the house, like a secret that had finally, exhaustedly, revealed itself to the most bored person in the world?

I placed the note back in the box, closed the lid, and gently settled the horse blanket over it. The heavy air of the guest room felt charged now, no longer empty. When I finally walked back into the living room, the dust motes were still dancing, but the lazy, sleepy quality of the afternoon was gone, replaced by a profound and specific wakefulness.

Shadows of our Love

It's strange how shadows lengthen just before sunset, how they stretch thin as though reluctant to leave the day behind. That's how I think of us—long and soft at the edges, fading but never quite gone.

I see you sometimes, not in person, but in the way certain things return. A woman laughing on a park bench. The smell of bergamot on someone's scarf. The sound of rain against a tin roof, steady and familiar, like your voice when you read aloud to me in the early years. The world has a way of looping back, replaying fragments of what it knows you can't let go.

We met on a train, or perhaps it was between stations. You had that impatient air of someone used to running late but pretending not to care. I was reading a novel—something about second chances—and you asked if it was any good. I said I hadn't decided yet. You said, "That's how I feel about Sydney." And that was it. I laughed. You smiled. Two people adrift, momentarily caught on the same tide.

In the months that followed, our love didn't burn fast or bright. It smouldered quietly, like a candle in a room no one else knew about. We met for coffee, which turned into walks, and walks that turned into hours. You told me about your job in advertising, how you hated selling things people didn't need. I told you about my father's garden, how he grew roses but refused to call them beautiful. "They're survivors," he'd say. You liked that. Said it sounded like me.

It wasn't passion that defined us—it was steadiness. You were the calm to my constant second-guessing, the reason I started believing mornings could mean something other than another day to endure. We built our life slowly: mismatched mugs, old records, the smell of burnt toast and fresh paint. Love, I learned, is not fireworks. It's the rhythm of ordinary days shared with the right person.

And then—life did what life does. It introduced cracks where none should not have been. I got the job in Melbourne. You stayed behind because your mother was sick. We told ourselves it was temporary. That love, genuine love, could survive distance. For a while, it did.

Our calls started strong—an hour, sometimes two, voices overlapping, laughing. Then came shorter calls, then texts, then the quiet spaces that neither of us filled. When I finally came back for a visit, I saw it in your eyes before you spoke. The fatigue of waiting, the subtle guilt of moving on. You said, "Maybe we've become more memory than motion." I nodded because I didn't know how to ask you to keep trying without sounding selfish.

We parted kindly, if such a thing exists. No slammed doors. No accusations. Just two people trying to let go of something that didn't want to be let go of.

Years passed. I built a new life, one that looked respectable from the outside—steady work, a modest apartment, someone to share meals with. Yet in the quiet hours, you'd return. Always gently. A thought, a scent, a line from a song. The human heart, I've learned, does not know finality. It archives what it loves and waits for the right light to bring it back into view.

Last month, I found one of your letters tucked inside a book I hadn't opened in years. The paper was yellowed; the ink was faint. You'd written: "If we ever meet again, I hope we recognise each other by kindness, not by regret."

I sat there for a long time, tracing the curve of your handwriting. I realised our story had never really ended—it had simply gone quiet. Perhaps that's what love does when it's too deep to die. It learns to live in silence.

Two weeks later, I saw you. By accident, or maybe by design—who can tell? I was in the city for a conference, crossing Hyde Park as the light fell. You were sitting on a bench, the same impatient tilt of your head, the same way of scanning the world as if you half-expected it to talk back.

I almost didn't approach. What good could come from reopening a wound that had learned to scar over neatly? But you looked up, and your eyes caught mine, and the years dissolved like sugar in tea.

"Still reading on trains?" You asked, smiling.

"Still pretending not to care when you're late?" I said.

We laughed. And in that moment, I felt it again—the calm warmth, the quiet recognition. Not the blaze of youth, but the steady glow of something enduring.

We walked. Talked about small things—work, health, the ridiculous rent prices. I learned you'd been married once, briefly. "Didn't last," you said, without bitterness. "He didn't like the silence."

We reached the fountain before the park lamps flickered on. The air smelled of jasmine. You turned to me and said, "Do you ever think about what might've been?"

"All the time," I said.

You nodded. "Me too. But maybe what we had was enough."

I wanted to say that enough is a strange word when it comes to love—that it can mean both peace and ache in the same breath. But I only smiled.

When we parted, you touched my sleeve lightly. No promises. No numbers exchanged. Just that small, human contact that says I remember.

Now, there are a few nights that I walk to the park and sit on that same bench. I then watch the shadows grow long and think of how love lingers.

Not always in grand gestures, but in the spaces between what was and what remains.

I learnt one thing: there are no saints in love, only witnesses.

We bear quiet testimony to what we've felt, to who we became because of it. You and I, we exist in that twilight— where memory and hope shake hands.

And when the light fades completely, I like to imagine our shadows still reaching for each other, stretching out across the years, reluctant to leave the day behind.

Because some loves don't end. Like me, they simply learn to live in a softer light.

The Unseen Truth

The memory shines, a diamond cut by time:
The summer I turned ten, at Grandpa's ancient farm.
The heat was thick; the air was sweet with pine,
And I, a king, am immune to any harm.

I picture sitting on his porch, sun-dazed,
Where woodbine curled and bees kept solemn pace.
And always, in that sun-struck, golden haze,
The perfect Orange Pop, held to my face.

It was a glass bottle, sweating cold and deep,
The colour of a sunset, fiercely bright.
I swear I hear the bottle cap release
That fizzy sound, a signal of delight.
He'd watch me drink, his eyes a gentle blue,
My favourite thing, a gift he always knew.

But then, last week, while cleaning out the shed,
I found the album—dusty, cracked, and old—
And flipped through the pages, full of things long dead,
The tale of that same summer to unfold.
There was the porch, the vine, the light, the same,
A picture labelled "Arthur, Age Ten."
I searched the frame, expecting liquid flame,
The orange glory of my memory then.

I see my hand grasping a sweating glass,
My face is blissful, truly, deeply pleased.
But there is no warm hue, no vibrant flash,
The liquid holds a yellow, sickly ease.
It's Lemony Fizz, the kind he always bought
For his own gout, a vile, cheap, pallid sort.

I never loved that stuff! It stung the tongue!
I'd beg for Orange, loud and full of spite!
The 'Pop' I loved, the one I praised and sung,
Was never his. It was the neighbour's, Dwight's.
He'd watch me drink the Lemon, plain and still,
And think his gift fulfilled my deepest will.

So, fifty years of perfect, golden ease,
A moment built on love and summer grace,
Was just a kid enduring, trying to please,
Drinking thin, tart yellow in that place.
My diamond memory, bright and finely wrought,
Turns out to be a sugar-free, yellow thought.
The love was real, but the drink? A cheap mistake.
And yet, for Grandpa's sake, I'll take it.

The Perils of Prophecy Management

The thing about being prophesied is that everyone focuses on the grand finale—the "slaying the Dark Lord" bit, or the "bringing peace to the Seven Realms" part.

Nobody, and I mean nobody, ever focuses on the highly embarrassing, deeply specific prerequisites.

My name is Harold, and according to the 7,000-year-old Scrolls of K'tharr, I was The One.

Unfortunately, the prophecy came with footnotes, and those footnotes were a disaster.

The relevant section read: "The hero, Harold, shall defeat the Shadow King, but only after he has (a) publicly mistaken a goat for his grandmother, (b) spilled an entire vat of artisanal sheep's milk cheese onto the Royal Guard Captain's boots, and (c) given a truly terrible, unsolicited performance of interpretive dance."

I read the prophecy, threw the scroll against a wall (it was surprisingly durable parchment), and went into full damage control mode.

The kingdom needed saving, yes, but my dignity needed saving more.

The goat incident, or 'Operation Grandma-Not-Goat,' was the first on the chopping block.

The prophecy didn't specify when this had to happen, only that it had to precede the last battle. I got it over with immediately, in the safest, most controlled environment possible: a small, isolated pen on a farm three villages away.

I found a goat named Agnes, a dignified creature with impeccable horns and surprisingly judgmental eyes. I pulled out my mobile phone to record the event for evidence (my attempts at proof had to be as ridiculous as the prophecy itself).

"Hello, Grandma!" I declared, trying to sound genuinely confused yet affectionate.

"You've lost weight! And gained several inches of wiry beard! Is that a new sweater? It smells faintly of grass and existential dread."

Agnes looked at me, chewed twice, and then head-butted the fence post I was leaning on. I achieved public humiliation, but not for the reason I intended.

The farmer, who had wandered out mid-speech, stared at the phone in my hand, then at the goat, then at me.

"Sir," he said slowly, "my wife has lived in the village for sixty years. She doesn't look like that. And she certainly doesn't chew on old tires."

"But the prophecy!" I pleaded.

"The prophecy says nothing about aggravated trespassing. Now move along, you goat-mistaking weirdo."

I had failed.

I had not mistaken the goat for my grandmother; I had simply been mistaken for a madman by a farmer.

I mentally crossed off (a) with a frustrated squiggle and moved on to the cheese.

The captain of the Royal Guard, a man named Gregor, was a towering mountain of impeccable polish and stern disapproval.

He wore boots so shiny you could see your reflection in them, which was exactly where the prophecy demanded the artisanal sheep's milk cheese land.

The cheese, a rare, runny, and pungently offensive Brie-like substance, was acquired. The plan: sneak into the mess hall, climb onto a chair, and "accidentally" drop the entire bucket onto his feet during the morning briefing.

I positioned myself precariously above Gregor, clutching the wooden bucket of sticky, aromatic disaster.

Gregor started discussing the supply lines.

This was my moment.

I leaned forward, ready to unleash the dairy avalanche.

"And finally," Gregor boomed, "I want to commend young Private Pringle, who, in a stunning display of foresight, noticed someone had placed a large, dripping pail of rancid dairy directly above my head."

I froze.

Private Pringle, a pale, pimply teen, winked at me.

"Yes, Pringle," Gregor continued, looking straight up at me with zero expression.

"This is a truly egregious security breach. Harold, I will give you two options: you can either drop that bucket and fulfill your bizarre destiny, or you can step down, put the bucket on the floor, and scrub every boot in this room until it sparkles, avoiding a court-martial for assault with a pungent weapon."

Defeated, I climbed down, placed the cheese on a nearby table, and spent three hours scrubbing the boots of men who kept calling me "The Dairy Disaster."

The worst part?

The entire vat of cheese accidentally tipped over when I tried to move it later, spilling directly onto a suit of armour worn by a different Captain, a visiting dignitary from the Empire of Atlantium which is a micro-nation and secular, pluralist progressive lobby group based in New South Wales, Australia.

It wasn't Gregor's boots, but it was close enough to be considered "Spilling an entire vat of artisanal cheese onto the Royal Guard Captain's equivalent," which, in the world of vague mysticism, probably counted.

Prophecy status: (a) Probably done, but unsatisfactorily. (b) Done, but on the wrong boots.

Which left (c): Interpretive Dance.

I am not a dancer. My body moves with the grace of a collapsing scaffolding rig. For my terrible, unsolicited performance, I chose "The Despair of Trying to Change Fate," performed in the middle of the village square during a quiet Tuesday afternoon.

I started with a sort of frantic flapping motion, representing the scroll throwing. Then came the rigid, robotic steps meant to embody my struggle against predestination. I concluded with a slow, agonizing crawl across the cobblestones, symbolizing my failed goat and cheese movements.

A crowd had gathered.

Mostly children and a few merchants were waiting for the weekly caravan. When I finally collapsed in a heap of metaphorical exhaustion, I looked up, expecting derision, maybe tomatoes.

Instead, a little girl clapped slowly. "Mommy," she whispered, loud enough for everyone to hear, "that man is doing a very, very bad impression of a giant, dying locust."

The entire town square erupted in laughter. It wasn't a sophisticated analysis of my movements; it was just honest, brutal, public humiliation.

It was without a doubt a truly terrible, unsolicited performance. I got up, dusted myself off, and retrieved the K'tharr scroll.

(a) Mistaking a goat for his grandmother: Check. (Farmer thought I was crazy, close enough.)

(b) Spilled cheese: Check. (Wrong captain, right amount of pungent chaos.)

(c) Interpretive dance: Double-check. (The dying locust.)

It turns out that fighting the minor, humiliating details of a prophecy is pointless because destiny, that cruel mistress, will simply find an adjacent, equally humiliating way to tick the boxes. I sighed, walked straight into the Shadow King's fortress (now that the preliminaries were out of the way), and defeated him in three minutes flat. It was the least dramatic, most professional part of my entire week.

I'm Harold, The Hero Who Smells Faintly of Rancid Brie and Moves Like a Dying Locust. You can call me The One. Just please don't ask me to dance.

The Mended Shawl

Clara sat by the bay window, the late afternoon sun casting long, dusty rectangles across the polished hardwood floor. The needles in her hands clicked with the gentle rhythm of a ticking clock, pulling a thread from a skein of soft, slate-grey yarn. She was finishing a shawl, a slow, deliberate task of mending not cloth, but time.

The colour, a shade she'd chosen for its quiet permanence, took her back forty years, to a bustling city street and a small, vibrant blue dress. It was the dress she'd worn every Tuesday night in the summer of 1978, the night she and Beatrice met for planning sessions.

Beatrice.

The name tasted like old wine and regret.

They had been inseparable in their twenties, bound by an obsessive, shared dream: to open a tiny, independent gallery on the coast. They'd spent months sketching layouts on napkins, hoarding vintage picture frames, and tasting lukewarm coffee in countless empty storefronts.

Their friendship was a vessel holding everything precious and fragile.

Their fears, their ambitions, and, most importantly, their pooled savings.

Clara remembered the sheer, giddy weight of the trust.

They had signed a partnership agreement on a sticky restaurant table, using a borrowed pen.

Beatrice, the more decisive of the two, had volunteered to handle the immediate finances—the lease deposit, the initial stock order.

"It's safer with me, Clarry," she'd said, tucking the cashier's check into her sensible leather briefcase, her smile bright and reassuring. "You worry too much."

Clara hadn't worried at all.

How could she?

Beatrice knew Clara's deepest truth: that building that gallery wasn't just a business plan; it was the foundation upon which Clara planned to build her adult life, a rebellion against the predictable path her family had laid out.

Beatrice knew this because Clara had told her everything, sharing the blueprints of her soul alongside the blueprints for the shop.

Then came the silence.

A week of unreturned calls became two weeks of rising panic.

A visit to Beatrice's apartment found it empty, the landlord confused, the briefcase gone.

The address for the intended gallery space now displayed a stern "Unavailable" sign.

The official letter arrived three weeks later, curt, and legalistic.

It was confirmed that Beatrice had used the funds to open a similar venture two states away, under her own name, taking full ownership of their initial stock and investment.

The note included was chillingly simple: "I needed a clean start more than you did. You'll be fine. Bea."

Clara closed her eyes, the rhythmic clicking of the needles pausing.

It was the raw, unadulterated shock that lingered after all these years, not just the financial loss, but the realisation that the shared reality she had lived in was a construct, carefully engineered to exploit her faith.

The sudden, agonizing collapse of belief was a deeper wound than the broken dream. She had loved Beatrice like a sister, sharing everything, including her most fragile dreams.

The perfidious friend betrayed their trust.

It took years to rebuild the financial stability, and even longer to let anyone hold her heart again without a fortress of doubt surrounding it. She never opened the gallery.

Instead, she became a meticulous, highly successful librarian, a woman who dealt only in solid facts and carefully categorised order. She surrounded herself with stories that had proper endings, unlike her own unexpected tragedy.

The betrayal had done more than steal money; it had taught her a profound, painful lesson in self-reliance. It forced her to stand completely alone, to define her worth without the mirror of a best friend reflecting an idealised version of herself.

Clara looked down at the shawl.

The last row was complete.

She snipped the yarn, pulling the loop tight.

The shawl was imperfect, with a knot here, a dropped stitch there, but it was warm, it was whole, and it was entirely her own creation.

It wasn't the beautiful, carefree garment she might have knitted in 1978, but it was the strong, resilient fabric of the woman she had become.

She draped it over her shoulders, feeling the weight of the years and the surprising, quiet comfort of a life she had to build for herself, stitch by painstaking stitch.

The Global Giggle and the Mosquito of 1998

My name is Arthur Pemble, and I am the most consequential idiot who ever lived. I didn't invent time travel; I didn't fail to save the world, and I certainly didn't press the big red button.

My crime was far, far pettier: I swatted a mosquito in 1997.

It's twenty-nine years later, and I'm standing in my kitchen, trying to make toast, while the entire city of Neo-Reading (and, I assume, the entire planet) engages in the Global Synchronization Jiggle.

The Jiggle is a compulsory, three-minute, high-energy dance routine broadcast every day at 8:05 AM, noon, and 5:00 PM.

It's accompanied by a relentless, synthesised electro-swing track called "Get Your Fiddle On, World!"

The music is loud, the steps are nonsensical, and, worst of all, the entire thing is mandatory via the Neural-Link Earbuds we all have to wear.

If you skip a single Jiggle, your bank account is frozen for 24 hours.

They call it "societal participation assurance."

I call it absolute tyranny.

I nearly dropped my toast when the chorus hit. I had to contort myself into the 'Wobbly Wombat' pose, one foot in the air, arms flapping like startled poultry, just as the automatic toaster tray popped out. The toast flew across the kitchen, bounced off the fridge, and landed directly in my dog Reginald's water bowl. Reginald, a creature of pure stoicism, didn't even flinch; he's used to the chaos.

This entire world, this absurd, dance-punishing nightmare, is my fault.

It all comes down to a hot July evening in 1998, specifically 5:58 PM, just before the local news started on Channel 7.

I was twenty-five, living in a dreary, carpeted flat, and I had two things going for me: a moderately impressive collection of pre-decimal coinage, and a pristine copy of The Economist.

I was scheduled to be interviewed on Reading Today for a two-minute segment on "Youthful Hobbies of Mild Interest."

It was my big shot at public recognition.

The phone rang.

It was Mr. Henderson, the segment producer. "Arthur, sorry, but we're pushing your slot back three minutes. You're now at 6:01 PM sharp. Be ready by the phone."

My stomach churned with nervous energy.

I had practiced my speech: "The 1923 penny, Mr Henderson, with its subtle obverse..."

Then, the beast appeared.

A mosquito.

Not just any mosquito. A buzzing, high-pitched, aggressively slow mosquito, determined to land exactly on my left forearm, which was resting perilously close to the old rotary phone that I still used as my landline.

I couldn't just swat it with my hand; that lacked precision.

I needed an instrument of lethal elegance.

I spotted The Economist.

Its stiffness and size were perfect.

To get the magazine, I had to execute what I now call The Flap.

I was sitting on a low, slightly wobbly stool.

The Economist was on a stack of encyclopedias beside me.

I decided that the safest, fastest way to grab the magazine without disturbing the phone was to:

Rotate my torso 45 degrees to the right.

Shift my weight completely to my right buttock.

Extend my left leg outwards to counter the torque.

Snatch the magazine in a swift, low arc.

I executed The Flap.

It was glorious.

The mosquito never saw it coming.

The magazine was in my hand; the stool hadn't tipped, and the insect was reduced to a smear of tiny injustice.

The only problem was the rotational shift in my weight (Step 2).

As I settled back onto the stool, I shifted my centre of gravity just two millimetres too far back.

The stool was already wobbly.

That tiny, two-millimetre over-shift caused the stool to wobble just enough that the phone, sitting on a high-pile rug, slid slightly on its worn rubber feet. The cord, which was taut, yanked the receiver off the hook.

I heard a dull thud as the receiver hit the carpet.

I lunged, picked it up, and fumbled to put it back down correctly.

It took four seconds.

Four seconds.

I had been so focused on the elegance of my mosquito assassination that I missed the crucial sound: the telephone ringing again.

It was Mr Henderson ringing at 6:00:58 PM.

He rang three times.

Since the receiver was off the hook, it went straight to an engaged signal (you remember those, right, reader?).

He waited thirty seconds, assumed I had bottled it, and called his backup segment.

The backup segment was about a mild-mannered man named Cecil who had successfully taught his parrot to recite Shakespeare.

Cecil's segment aired.

Now, here is where the causality chain becomes a comedic masterpiece of horror.

A prominent venture capitalist named Baroness Tilda Grimshaw was watching Reading Today.

She was ready to invest her entire fund—$800 million—into a new, groundbreaking, and revolutionary technology.

She was looking for signs of intellectual curiosity, attention to detail, and nonconformity.

She wasn't watching for my coin segment, though.

She was watching for the segment after mine.

The segment is about a revolutionary product called the Hush-Vac.

The Hush-Vac was a vacuum cleaner so silent it could operate while a baby slept. It would have transformed domestic life, ushering in an era of quiet, meditative cleaning and global peace. The Hush-Vac founder was due to be on at 6:04 PM.

Baroness Grimshaw had a secret signal: if the interviewee before the Hush-Vac segment showed a specific type of neurotic passion, the kind displayed by someone obsessing over pre-decimal pennies, she would know the time was right.

She believed in patterns.

But she didn't see my neurotic passion for pennies.

She saw Cecil's parrot squawking out Hamlet's soliloquy.

"Neurotic passion," she muttered, "but insufficient."

In a fit of pique, Baroness Grimshaw immediately called her broker and pulled her funding from the Hush-Vac.

Instead, she invested $800 million into the next thing on her investment spreadsheet: a company founded by a man named Gary Glum. Gary Glum's company was called Rhythmic Pebble, Inc.

Their product: a new, app-enabled version of the Pet Rock, except this one vibrated silently at preset intervals.

The Hush-Vac company denied the capital, folded in 1998.

The world was forever doomed with loud, annoying vacuum cleaners.

But Rhythmic Pebble, Inc. (RPI)? It was a runaway success.

People loved their silently vibrating stones.

Gary Glum became the richest man on Earth.

Gary Glum wasn't just a tech mogul; he was an obsessed, lifelong fan of musical theatre and synchronised movement. In 2018, having bought every major media and infrastructure company, he used his wealth and influence to enact his terrifying vision for "A More Harmonious Earth."

He retired the old national anthem.

He banned competitive sports.

He replaced the entire school curriculum with mandatory tap-dance lessons. And most importantly, he instituted the Global Synchronization Jiggle.

He even commissioned the infuriating electro-swing track, "Get Your Fiddle On, World!"

The Jiggle isn't just a dance; it's a constant, noisy reminder of the silent world that might have been. A world where I could have cleaned my flat in peace, a world without Wobbly Wombats and flapping poultry arms.

I finally fished my soggy toast out of Reginald's bowl, the last vestiges of "Get Your Fiddle On, World!" fading into the distance.

The clock reads 6:08 AM.

The silence is deafening, punctuated only by the drip of dog-water from my slice of bread.

I walk over to the window, look out at the newly quiet streets, and watch a sanitation worker begin his shift.

The sanitation truck roars past, its engine painfully loud, because silent vacuum technology never evolved. It was killed by a parrot, whose owner only appeared on TV because I shifted my weight two millimetres to avoid a mosquito.

I lift my hand, ready to smash the Neural-Link Earbud out of frustration but stop.

I've learned my lesson.

Every infinitesimal movement, every single flap, has a cost.

The last time I tried to eliminate an annoying pest, I ruined the future.

Maybe I think I should just go back to my coin collection.

It's quiet, it's safe, and the only potential butterfly effect it might cause is an existential crisis for a tax auditor.

And frankly, they probably deserve it.

The Weight of What is Enough

The rain started not with a dramatic crash, but with a soft, insistent whisper against the windowpane. It was the kind of July rain that demanded a blanket, a strong cup of tea and coffee, and permission to pause.

I watched the drops race each other down the glass, the city lights blurring into watercolour streaks outside our third-floor unit.

Robert was on the old velvet sofa, half-hidden behind a stack of graphic novels, but I could hear the rhythmic rustle of the pages turning. He looked up when I placed two steaming mugs on the coffee table — mine Earl Grey, his just strong black coffee with a splash of milk.

"You're brooding, aren't you?" he asked, his voice low and warm, setting his book down on his chest.

I smiled faintly, settling beside him and pulling the worn cashmere throw over my legs. "Not brooding, exactly. Just thinking about all the things, we haven't done."

He waited, knowing where my mind often wandered.

I thought about the glossy magazine articles I'd read.

Couples conquering Kilimanjaro, building houses on remote coasts, launching world-changing tech startups. We were twenty-nine, not backpacking through Asia, not closing multi-million-dollar deals.

We were just here, with chipped mugs, a struggling basil plant, and rent due on Friday.

"We never took that trip to Patagonia," I admitted, tracing the rim of my mug. "And my novel is still just three chapters and a very detailed mood board."

Robert reached out, his hand finding mine under the blanket, his thumb brushing over my knuckles.

"And how is that bad, exactly?"

"It feels small. Maybe we settled for the safe path instead of the brave one. We built this perfectly quiet little world when we were supposed to be out conquering the loud one."

He squeezed my hand.

"The loud one is overrated, Emily. It's expensive, and it has terrible parking."

He laughed, the sound easy and genuine.

He tilted his head, looking past the rain to the cozy confines of our living room: the bookshelf bowed under the weight of years, the mismatched cushions, the small fire flickering comfortingly in the fireplace.

"All those grand adventures we planned when we were twenty-one," I murmured. "They felt like prerequisites for a good life."

Robert shifted, pulling me closer until my head rested on his shoulder.

His presence was an anchor, steady, and comforting.

The rain seemed to dim the entire world outside, amplifying the warmth within our four walls. I inhaled the familiar scent of his jumper, wool, and Acqua di Gio, and let the weight of ambition settle away.

And then the truth hit me.

I realised that the peace of this predictable evening felt like a victory in itself.

We shared silence.

Our knowledge that we would wake up next to each other and navigate another ordinary Tuesday.

I smiled, knowing that the grand, sweeping gestures I once craved now seemed thin and exhausting compared to this deep, durable contentment.

Gently I lean into him and close my eyes, and let the quiet conclusion form in my mind, a gentle sigh of relief.

Perhaps we have what we need.

Waves Are Like Whispers

I always thought Greece would smell like olives and sea salt. Turns out, it smells like sunscreen, diesel from the ferry, and something sweet—maybe honey dripping from a baklava shop on the pier.

It's my first time out of Australia, my first stamp in the passport Dad gave me on my seventeenth birthday.

He said, "Go find something beautiful and make it part of who you are." I think he got that line from a movie, but I didn't correct him.

Mum and I are doing this trip together.

Her idea mostly. "A mother–daughter adventure," she called it.

I think she needed it more than I did.

It's been two years since Dad passed, and she's been trying to fill the house with plans—renovations, courses, and now this trip.

I didn't want to come at first.

Leaving his memory behind, even for a few weeks, felt like cheating on him. But when I saw her scrolling through pictures of Santorini at midnight, eyes wet and dreamy, I said yes.

The ferry rocks like a lullaby gone wrong.

Everyone seems relaxed. Couples leaning into each other, kids eating chips, a man playing a bouzouki—but my stomach flips with every wave.

Mum's at the railing, taking photos, her hair blowing wildly.

I'm sitting cross-legged on the deck, sketching the horizon.

I've started drawing again, something I hadn't done since before Dad got sick.

A boy of about my age passes by, holding a paper cone of roasted chestnuts.

He stops and looks at my sketchbook. "That's good," he says in accented English. "The sea. You make it look as if it's moving."

I laugh.

"Maybe because the boat's moving."

He grins.

"Still, you see it right. Most people just draw blue."

His name's Nikos.

He's from Athens, going to visit his grandparents on Paros.

He tells me about how his grandfather used to fish every morning before sunrise, how his grandmother still makes bread in a clay oven that's older than anyone in the village. "You should come by," he says. "See the real Greece, not the postcard one."

Mum catches my eye from the railing.

I wave. She waves back, smiling that soft, tired smile she's worn since Dad died—the one that never quite reaches her eyes.

Paros looks like someone spilled white paint on a mountain and called it a town. The houses gleam in the sunlight, blue shutters blinking like sleepy eyes.

We rent a room with a small balcony overlooking the sea.

Mum unpacks while I wander down to the beach with my sketchbook.

The sand is rougher than I expected, full of tiny pebbles that sparkle like broken glass.

The water, though—it's another world.

Transparent and endless.

I wade in up to my knees and feel the chill bite into my skin.

A voice behind me says, "You came."

It's Nikos, holding two bottles of orange soda. He sits beside me, offering one. "For courage," he says.

We talk for hours about school, about music, about how strange it is to grow up and realise your parents are just people.

He wants to study marine biology.

I told him I'm not sure what I want yet, but I like the idea of stories—how they outlast everything else.

When the sun sets, the sky turns peach and violet.

He asks if he can take a photo of me sketching.

I nod, pretending to focus on the drawing, but really, I'm trying not to blush. The air smells of salt and thyme.

Somewhere, I hear a dog barking.

The next day we spent exploring the town, exploring the narrow alleyways, and laughing at the cats as they napped on doorsteps, and were in awe as we saw old women selling handmade lace with the brightest smiles on their faces. Mum buys a small silver bracelet shaped like waves.

"For you," she says. "A reminder that life keeps moving."

That evening, we have dinner at a taverna by the water.

There's music, laughter, the clatter of plates. I see Nikos across the square with his grandparents.

He waves; I wave back. Mum notices and raises an eyebrow. "A friend?"

"Sort of," I say, playing with my fork. "He's from Athens."

"Ah," she teases. "The plot thickens."

We both laugh.

It's the first time in months I've seen her laugh properly.

For a moment, I think Dad would've liked this—seeing us like this, alive again.

A few days later, Nikos took me on a bike ride along the coast.

The air rushes past my face, warm and free.

We stop at a cliff overlooking the sea. Below us, waves crash against the rocks, spraying white foam.

"This is where my grandfather used to fish," he says. "He'd say the sea knows every secret but never tells."

I nod, watching the water glitter. "Maybe it tells in its own way. Waves are like whispers."

He looks at me and smiles. "You think too much."

"Maybe."

We sit in silence.

Then he reaches out, brushes a strand of hair from my face. My heart stumbles in my chest. The world narrows to the sound of the sea and his hand hovering near mine.

He leans closer, but I turn slightly, pretending to point at the horizon. "Look," I say softly. "A sailboat."

He smiles, understanding. He doesn't push it. And somehow, that makes it even more real.

That night, back on our balcony, I tell Mum about the day—well, most of it.

She listens, half-asleep, her feet up on the railing. "You sound happy," she murmurs.

"I am," I say.

And I mean it.

Later, when she goes to bed, I stay outside.

The moon hangs low, orange, and heavy. I open my sketchbook.

On one page, I draw the sea; on the next, I draw a pair of hands almost touching.

Our last day arrives too soon.

Mum wants to visit a monastery on the hill. Nikos meets us halfway up the path with a small box in his hand. Inside is a tiny seashell strung on a bit of leather.

"A piece of the Aegean," he says. "So, you don't forget."

I give him my drawing of the sea. "So, you remember," I say.

He laughs. "You make it sound like we'll never meet again."

"Maybe we won't," I reply.

"But that's okay. Some people belong to moments, not lifetimes."

He looks at me for a long time before saying, "Then this was a good moment."

The flight back to Sydney feels longer than it did going there.

Mum sleeps most of the way. I stare out the window; the clouds rolling like marble beneath us. I take out the seashell, feeling its smooth edge.

It's strange how quickly places attach themselves to you.

Greece wasn't just a trip—it was like waking up after a long sleep.

I thought I'd left home to escape the grief, but instead, I found a way to live with it.

When we land, the air feels heavier, thicker.

Mum stretches, yawns. "Back to reality," she says.

I smile and add. "Maybe a better version of it."

A few weeks later, I'm sitting by the lake near our house in Northport, sketching again.

The afternoon light shimmers across the water. I open my sketchbook and find the page with the hands almost touching. Beneath it, I write:

"The sea knows every secret but never tells."

I can still hear the waves, still taste the salt.

Sometimes, I catch Mum looking at me as if she's trying to figure out what changed. I don't tell her that part of me is still sitting on a sun-warmed cliff in Paros, listening to a boy named Nikos talk about the sea.

Because maybe that's what growing up is—not holding on but carrying things differently. Like how the sea carries every pebble it's ever touched, smoothing them with time.

And maybe that's what Dad meant when he said, "Go find something beautiful and make it part of who you are."

The Ballad of Bartholomew Buttercup

Bartholomew Buttercup was, by all accounts, a perfectly respectable man. He possessed a respectable job (assistant regional accountant for a mid-tier stationery supplier in New South Wales), a respectable unit in Northport (third floor, facing a respectable brick wall), and a respectable, if entirely uneventful, life.

But beneath the veneer of beige respectability, a seismic craving rumbled. Bartholomew lived with a profound, aching yearning for something he had lost years ago, a loss so deep it had carved a gluten-free, whole-wheat-rice-cracker-shaped hole in his soul.

Bartholomew had celiac disease.

Not the trendy 'Oh, I'm just watching my carbs' kind.

The bona fide, 'A single breadcrumb could send me to the emergency room in a fiery chariot of agony' kind. For years, he'd been a silent martyr in a world dripping with delicious, doughy temptation.

Every waft from a pizza place was a siren song of despair. Every supermarket bread aisle was a cathedral of exquisite, inedible architecture.

His yearning wasn't for a specific person, or a dream job, or a secluded cottage. His yearning was for 'The Perfect Baguette'. He dreamed of it.

A baguette with a crust so shattering it sounded like dry leaves underfoot, giving way to a springy, airy interior, its flavour a complex, yeasty symphony of simple ingredients. He yearned to simply *tear* a piece off, dip it in olive oil, and experience the simple, perfect pleasure of normal human consumption.

He had a shrine in his apartment – a modest, well-lit shelf above his certified-safe rice flour blend. On it sat a single, magnificent, three-day-old baguette he had bought for purely observational purposes. It was stale, hard as concrete, and utterly untouchable, but Bartholomew would gaze upon it with the wistful reverence of a lover separated by war.

"Oh, *Henri*," he'd whisper, giving the baguette a name, a little piece of dignity in its inedible afterlife. "You are a magnificent, inflammatory beast. What I wouldn't give for just a moment of your company!"

His therapist, Dr. Vivian Quirk, suggested he try visualisation.

"Bartholomew," she'd said, tapping her pen against her organic kale smoothie. "When the craving hits, visualize the *feeling* of satisfaction, not the food itself. Picture a calm, fulfilled stomach."

Bartholomew tried.

The next time he passed a bakery and inhaled the intoxicating aroma of freshly baked sourdough, he closed his eyes and tried to visualise a 'calm, fulfilled stomach.'

Instead, his mind conjured an image of his stomach wearing a tiny Viking helmet, furiously batting away miniature, animated loaves of bread with a sword made of celery.

The visualisation was a spectacular, if counterproductive, failure.

His friends, well-meaning but utterly insensitive, only made it worse.

"Dude, this pretzel is *epic*," his colleague, Gary, once announced, brandishing a jumbo, salt-encrusted twist inches from Bartholomew's face. "You know, the gluten-free ones just don't have that *chew*, man. It's a texture thing."

Bartholomew's inner Viking stomach went full berserker.

He simply smiled a strained, fixed smile and changed the subject to quarterly projections.

The pinnacle of his yearning came during his annual holiday trip to Paris.

He went not for the museums or the romance, but purely for the sheer, unadulterated *density* of gluten in the atmosphere.

He spent his first morning sitting at a pavement café, nursing a safe black coffee, and simply *watching*.

He watched a tiny, elegant woman casually snapping off the end of a croissant.

He watched a construction worker demolishing a jambon-beurre sandwich with gusto.

He watched a pigeon peck at a discarded piece of brioche, and for a fleeting, terrifying second, he felt a flicker of envy for the pigeon.

That afternoon, he found it.

Tucked away on a side street was *Le Pain Merveilleux*.

And in its window, resting on a velvet pillow (or so it seemed to his inflamed imagination) was the platonic ideal of a baguette.

It was perfect.

Golden, ridged, and arrogant in its deliciousness.

Bartholomew felt a dizzying combination of desire and despair.

He walked into the shop.

The air was thick and sweet, a lethal vapor of wheat flour.

"Bonjour," he squeaked to the baker, a man whose forearms were the size of small hams, dusted with white powder.

"Bonjour, monsieur. Un baguette? Une tradition?"

Bartholomew swallowed, his throat dry. He looked at the perfect baguette. He looked at the baker. He looked at the inevitable, agonizing consequences.

"I would like to purchase your most beautiful baguette," Bartholomew announced, his voice trembling with the weight of the moment. "But please place it immediately in a sealed bag. Two bags, actually. And for the love of all that is holy, do not let it touch my hands. Use the tongs."

The baker, a Parisian veteran of human eccentricity, raised a single, flour-dusted eyebrow but complied.

Bartholomew paid, gingerly accepting the double-bagged sacred object.

He carried it back to his hotel room like a priceless, volatile artefact. He placed it on the desk. He locked the door.

He spent the next two hours simply smelling it.

He would crack open the first bag just enough for a single, intoxicating sniff of pure, yeast-driven perfection.

The aroma was everything he had dreamed of warm, earthy, heavenly.

He inhaled deeply, his eyes watering, a small, choked sob escaping his lips.

It was the closest he would ever get.

When his two hours were up, when the glorious scent had faded slightly, and his willpower had reached its absolute limit, Bartholomew did the only thing a respectable, Celiac-stricken man in Paris could do.

He called room service and politely asked them to take away the dangerous, inflammatory, and utterly magnificent evidence. As the waiter left with the double-bagged treasure, Bartholomew sat down, took a deep breath, and opened a packet of his emergency, gluten-free, individually wrapped corn crackers.

"One day, Henri," he whispered, gazing mournfully at the empty spot on the desk. "One day, a scientist will invent a gluten antidote, and we shall be reunited."

He bit into the cracker.

It tasted, as always, of disappointment and dry cardboard.

But underneath the profound yearning, a small, respectable voice reminded him: *At least you didn't need the emergency room.*

The yearning remained, of course.

It was now simply seasoned with the exquisite, maddening memory of the most beautiful scent in the world.

And that, Bartholomew realised, was perhaps the saddest and funniest part of all.

The Chorus of Newport

We are the Chorus. We are the Shadow. We are the perpetual rustling counter-narrative to the quiet life of Northport, NSW.

Our domain is not the neatly mown grass or the double-garage homes; it is the infrastructure above—the swaying power lines, the dense crowns of the jacaranda trees, and the expansive, limitless sky. From these lofty seats, we oversee the routine, the petty, and the deeply private lives of the bipedal creatures below.

We are judges, critics, and relentless commentators.

We never stop talking.

The most reliable performers in our daily show were the old couple.

We referred to them amongst ourselves in a rapid, staccato dialect that sounded like stones rattling down a drainpipe—as The Bright-Foot and The Slow-Knees.

The Bright-Foot was a woman, always wearing sneakers in startling hues of magenta or electric blue, moving with a quick, decisive energy, leading the way.

The Slow-Knees was the man, shambling slightly, wearing the same terrible, faded blue cap every day, and always by her side.

Their path was fixed: down the crescent by the park at 8:05 AM, turning left onto the street where the enormous, drought-resistant succulents grew, and back home by 8:45 AM, no matter the weather.

We learned to set our own internal clocks by their gait.

"Look at The Slow-Knees today," croaked Krrk, our oldest and most merciless observer, perched on the highest tension wire.

"He is wearing the brown shorts again. The ones that bunch at the waist. A failure of tailoring, surely."

Caw! came the consensus from the lower branches.

Caw, caw, a failure!

"And the Bright-Foot," chimed in Scylla, the one with the damaged left wing who preferred to patrol the lower eaves. "She is talking to him about the lawn again. Listen! *'—too high, Gerald! I specifically said to set the blades higher.'* Such dedication to grass management. We should drop a twig on her head. Just one."

We never dropped a twig.

Our game was observation and vocal critique, not active sabotage.

We had a code of conduct: never interfere, only narrate.

And our narration was loud.

It was a cacophony of detailed judgment, running commentary on their outfits, their posture, the contents of the dog-waste bags they carried, the fragments of human conversation that drifted up to us.

"He coughed twice at the corner—is that a sign of weakness? Will the Slow-Knees fail to complete the circuit today? We should take bets."

"Her sunglasses are crooked. Crooked! Does she not see the world at an angle? Does he not care enough to straighten them for her?"

"They are holding hands today. They did not hold hands yesterday. What is the significance of this deviation? Analyse. Discuss. Be louder!"

Our collective noise, the rolling, relentless *caw-caw-KRRR-krrk-CROW!* of our ongoing debate and gossip, was a constant, almost physical thing.

It was the background static of the Northport dawn, and we assumed, as we always had, that the humans simply registered it as part of the indifferent natural world—a noise without meaning, certainly without hostile *intent*.

Then came the morning everything changed.

They were rounding the corner by the enormous brick wall, and The Bright-Foot was speaking rapidly, her voice a tense high wire.

The Slow-Knees was shrugging, stuffing his hands deep into his pockets. It seemed they were having a disagreement, maybe about that cursed lawn, maybe something heavier.

The air was thick with the silent tension that humans carry, but our Chorus, sensing drama, only increased the volume. We were a flock of critical eyes, screaming our interpretations.

"She is frowning! Look at the fold between her eyes! He has certainly forgotten an important date! He is guilty! He looks entirely guilty!"

"He is picking at a thread on his shirt. A displacement activity! We should scream his failures louder!"

We reached a fever pitch, an overwhelming storm of caws and croaks, close enough to be heard over the rush of a passing ute.

The Bright-Foot suddenly stopped dead.

The Slow-Knees stopped as well, startled.

She stopped.

She didn't look down at the pavement, or at her husband, or at the trees generally.

She looked *up*.

She looked directly into the jacaranda crown where Krrk and I were perched. She looked right at us, or rather, *through* the leaves, directly at the source of the noise.

And then she spoke.

But she wasn't speaking to The Slow-Knees, or to the world, or to herself.

Her voice was sharp, clear, and projected upward, cutting through the entire racket.

"Oh, for heaven's sake," she snapped, her face etched with exasperation, not fear. "You loud-mouthed lot! We can barely hear ourselves think. Keep it down!"

A collective hush fell upon The Chorus.

It was instantaneous.

The silence was so sudden and profound that it felt like the earth itself had stopped spinning.

We didn't move.

We didn't breathe.

She heard us.

She hadn't just registered 'crow noise.'

She had registered *us*.

She knew we were talking. She knew the noise was directed.

She understood it was a deliberate, concentrated vocal act.

In the Chorus's history, across generations of observation, no human had ever broken the Fourth Wall like that.

No one had acknowledged our conversation.

She treated us not like wildlife, but like a bunch of ill-mannered neighbours yelling over the fence.

The Slow-Knees, completely oblivious, gently touched her shoulder.

"Come on, dear. Don't worry about the crows. They're just crows."

The Bright-Foot just shook her head, gave us one last, withering glare, a look that said, *'I know you're in there, and I know you're gossiping,'* and continued her walk.

We were chastened.

We were silent.

And more than that, we were deeply, profoundly impressed.

The Bright-Foot had earned our grudging corvid respect.

We never forgot that moment.

For weeks afterward, our commentary, while still constant, was muted whenever they passed.

We spoke in hushed, respectful clicks and whispers until they were well out of earshot.

The daily walk became strangely peaceful.

The season turned.

The brilliant purple jacaranda flowers came and went, replaced by the deep green of summer, and then the dry, ochre tones of a mild autumn in New South Wales.

It had been several months since The Bright-Foot had silenced The Chorus.

One morning, our internal clock ticked 8:05 AM.

We waited.

Only The Slow-Knees appeared.

He was wearing the same terrible blue cap, but it sat differently now, tilted slightly, as if carelessly tossed onto his head.

His pace was slower, more listless. He was still The Slow-Knees, but now he was The Alone.

We searched the park gates, the corners, the side paths.

No Bright-Foot.

The next day, the same.

And the next.

Our silence from the scolding now felt oppressive.

We watched The Alone wander, and his movements became more erratic. He wasn't just walking; he was *acting*.

He would stop by the large succulent, wave his hand dismissively into the empty air beside him, and say clearly: "But it's just so much easier to get the milk from the smaller shop, Margaret. You know that."

He was arguing with the space where The Bright-Foot should have been.

He was walking with the weight of invisible companionship, reliving the petty debates, the small, constant negotiations of a long marriage.

The grief was a visible shroud wrapped around him, heavy and grey. He wasn't just mourning; he was keeping her alive by debating her ghost.

Our sophisticated corvid understanding of human ritual and possession told us the truth immediately: The Bright-Foot was gone.

The silence she had commanded from us now felt wrong—an active neglect. We realised our silence, once a sign of respect, had become just another space in his life.

He was alone, and he was breaking.

The Chorus convened.

Our meeting was serious, conducted in low, solemn clicks, and head tilts.

We must intervene.

We who judged his gait, his cap, his posture, now see a deeper failure. A failure of the system.

He has lost his routine, his counterargument, his Bright-Foot.

We shall become the new routine. We shall become The Soft-Foot.

Our task was not to replace her, but to gently chaperone him through the worst of his solitude.

The first step was to break the monotony of the path that now only held painful memories.

We used our collective body to guide him.

As The Alone approached the corner where he always turned left, the corner that led back to the quiet house, five of us suddenly swooped low, landing on the pavement ten yards ahead, perfectly spaced.

We didn't caw.

We simply stared at him, then simultaneously hopped toward the right, down the narrow, sun-dappled lane he never used.

He stopped mid-step, looking at the road, then at us.

He paused, waved his hand in a small, internal gesture (perhaps The Bright-Foot's disagreement), and then, with a heavy sigh, he followed us.

The new lane led to a cul-de-sac bordered by an old farm wall overgrown with ivy and climbing roses—a path with fresh smells and new distractions.

We led him slowly, maintaining the lead, forcing his eyes to look at the textures of the wall, the patterns of the light, the unfamiliar sight of a cat in a window.

We did this for a week.

He never acknowledged our guidance, but he always followed the new path.

Then came the gifts.

We knew The Slow-Knees appreciated the mundane.

He often picked up strange little pieces of pavement detritus, a smooth stone, a colourful strip of plastic, only to drop them again.

We formalised this ritual.

Near the gate of his return, just where the footpath met the driveway, we began leaving small, carefully selected items. Krrk, who was the best hunter of trash, found a piece of sea-blue glass, smoothed by something, perhaps a lawnmower, and laid it gently in a clear patch of dirt. Scylla found a shiny, slightly crumpled foil wrapper from a chocolate bar, dazzling in the morning light, and placed it next to the glass. I contributed a perfect miniature white feather.

He found the collection the next day.

He stopped at the gate, looked down, and then knelt slowly, creakily, to examine them.

He didn't pick them up immediately.

He just stared.

We watched from the rooftop across the road, silent and attentive.

Then, The Alone reached out, picking up the sea-blue glass.

He rubbed it between his fingers. A tiny, almost imperceptible smile touched the corners of his mouth. The first true smile we had seen on him since The Bright-Foot had vanished.

He slipped the glass into the pocket of his shorts, leaving the feather and the foil.

The next day, the gifts were replenished.

A bright orange marble.

A perfect, symmetrical twig.

We didn't talk anymore during his walks.

The loud, judgmental Chorus had dissolved, replaced by a silent, protective vigil.

We would perch, a silent black flock, scattered ahead of him on the wires and branches, simply *watching*.

He still talked to the space beside him, arguing about the price of petrol, complaining about the neighbour's dog, making observations about the quality of the coffee.

But now, when he rounded the corner, instead of a void of sound, he had The Shadow.

He didn't need us to talk.

He needed an audience.

He needed the validation of a routine being maintained, even if he was only half of the pair.

He needed to know that some ancient, knowing presence was still there, observing his new life, witnessing his grief, and quietly, non-judgementally, providing him with a handful of sea-blue glass and a slightly altered path toward the rising sun.

We were The Chorus.

We would never stop observing.

But we had learned a new language of companionship: the sound of respectful silence, the glint of a found treasure, and the shared understanding between a man in a terrible blue hat and the murder of crows who knew everything about him.

The walks continued.

And we were always there.

We were his quiet, new routine, waiting for him every morning in Northport, NSW.

The Relic of Blackwood Manor

It was a dark and stormy night. Rain lashed against the cracked windowpanes of Blackwood Manor with the sound of a thousand frantic claws, and the wind howled a monotonous, chilling dirge through the chimney stacks.

Elias Thorne, the manor's reluctant new owner, stood in the dust-choked library, the flickering beam of his flashlight barely conquering the overwhelming darkness. He had inherited this ruinous estate from a distant, unknown relative, and while the will promised wealth, the atmosphere promised only terror.

Elias wasn't here for the inheritance, though.

He was here because of a small, cryptic diary entry he had found belonging to his grandmother, referencing "the Blackwood curse" and a need to prevent someone from digging up the past.

That phrase had clung to his mind, pulling him across three states to this forgotten corner of the world.

He was determined to understand the silence that had always surrounded his family's history.

The air in the house was heavy, smelling of decay, mildew, and something else, something metallic, like the old, discontinued Aussie one-cent piece made of copper and cold fear.

He navigated by instinct through the ground floor; past portraits whose eyes seemed to follow the storm's shifting light.

His search eventually led him to the study, a small room tucked behind a massive tapestry, which was the only area of the house the lawyers had not picked clean.

There against the far wall stood a wardrobe, an antique monstrosity made of black, heavily carved oak. It was sealed not with a lock, but with heavy chains wrapped tightly around its girth, fastened by a naval grade padlock whose iron was fused with rust.

It pulsed with a cold energy that made the hair on Elias's arms stand rigid.

This was where the history was buried.

This was the place his grandmother had warned him against.

He spent an hour sawing through the chains with a rusty tool he found in the potting shed; the storm swallowed almost instantly the grinding metal sound. As the last link broke, the padlock fell, striking the floor with a dead thud.

He pulled the heavy double doors open.

The immediate smell that rushed out was overwhelming. It was like a blast of graveyard earth, formaldehyde, and something sharply acrid, like burnt sugar. Elias recoiled, coughing, but his curiosity was a burning compulsion.

Inside, there were no clothes, no moth-eaten furs.

The wardrobe was lined entirely in black felt and mounted on the back wall were three items: a tarnished silver locket containing a lock of black hair; a thick leather-bound book written in Latin; and, hanging from a rusted hook, a blood-stained rope.

It was the book that confirmed his greatest fears about the manor and his lineage.

He took it out, laying it on the desk.

The cover was cold to the touch.

The text was a meticulous, chilling chronicle, detailing generations of a single-family tradition: maintaining the "Relic of Blackwood."

As he read the spidery script, a creeping realisation dawned: the family didn't just *have* secrets; the secrets *were* the family.

The journal chronicled how the patriarchs of the manor, generation after generation, had dealt with the true cost of their family's influence: the human sacrifices required to keep the manor's "luck."

The journal detailed the names, dates, and gruesome specifics of those who had to be 'retired' to maintain the power.

Elias suddenly understood the saying, not as a metaphor, but as a literal accounting of the horrific inheritance he now faced.

The history of Blackwood Manor was figuratively full of skeletons in the closet.

As Elias reached the last entry, dated 1963, a noise made him drop the book.

It wasn't the wind, nor the rain.

It was a dry, shuffling scrape directly behind him.

He spun around, the torch beam shaking wildly.

The back wall of the closet, which he had thought was the solid, felt-lined back of the wardrobe, was now sliding inward with a grating sound.

A low, guttural moan echoed from the space beyond.

Elias shone the light into the gaping hole.

It was a narrow, dusty crawl space, and in the centre, chained to the damp floor, was the Relic itself.

It was a partially preserved human torso, desiccated and horrifying, adorned with brittle ceremonial ribbons.

This was the source of the metallic, acrid smell.

But the Relic was not alone.

Hovering just above it, partially visible in the dim light, was a figure.

Tall, gaunt, and impossibly pale, dressed in the rotting finery of a long-dead era. Its eyes, deep sockets of shadow and rage, fixed on Elias.

The figure reached out a hand, its fingers impossibly long and tipped with broken nails.

"You came to look," the creature rasped, its voice like sand and broken glass. "You came to own. You came to continue the line."

Elias stumbled backward, his heart hammering against his ribs, finally understanding that the true secret wasn't the documents he'd read, but the living, breathing, spectral horror it contained.

Digging up the past had not set him free; it had merely activated the curse, making him the newest victim, or the newest unwilling caretaker.

The storm outside seemed to scream its approval, welcoming him to his eternal role in the black history of Blackwood Manor.

The Gloom of the Gurnard

Arthur Ponsonby, literary agent, and patron saint of the terminally disheartened, regarded the man in his waiting area with the detached sorrow usually reserved for watching a particularly slow-moving iceberg melt.

The man's name was, impossibly, Vinnie "The Viz" Visconte.

Vinnie was wearing a suit the colour of the now old, discontinued Australian one-cent coin, a shirt unbuttoned to a depth that suggested a hasty departure from a yacht, and a gold chain chunky enough to anchor a small dinghy.

He radiated an energy that smelled faintly of cheap cologne, desperation, and aggressively implemented market synergy.

"Mr. Visconte is here to see you about Agnes Periwinkle," Arthur's assistant, a perpetually exhausted drama student named Chloe, whispered over the intercom.

Agnes Periwinkle.

Dear sweet Agnes.

The author of seventeen novels about elderly sea witches and their emotionally stunted amphibian companions, most famously *The Gloom of the Gurnard*.

Agnes, who had shuffled off this mortal coil three weeks ago after a tragic incident involving a crocheted blanket, an overly enthusiastic tabby cat, and a flight of stairs.

Arthur sighed, a sound worn smooth by years of dealing with erratic authors and even more erratic film producers.

"Send in the... Viz," he instructed.

Vinnie erupted into the office with the kinetic force of a dropped toolbox. He didn't shake hands; he enveloped Arthur's hand in a clammy, diamond-encrusted grip and pumped it once, violently.

"Arthur! Pleasure, pleasure. Look, I'm going to cut the small talk, right? I've seen the numbers on *Gurnard*. It's a sleeper, a *masterpiece*, but it's got a visibility problem. A massive visibility problem. We're talking IP, Arthur. Intellectual property. And I've got the vision."

Arthur carefully retrieved his hand, checking if his wedding ring was still there. "That's very observant, Mr. Visconte. Agnes had a loyal following, but yes, her oeuvre was, shall we say, niche?"

"Niche is just undersold, Arthur! Niche is just a cinematic experience waiting for a green light!"

Vinnie pulled up a chair uninvited, reversing it and straddling the backrest like a cowboy who'd wandered into a board meeting.

He produced a heavily branded phone from his pocket.

"I've got to tell you, Arthur, my business model, it's not just a service, it's a *philosophy*. It's about taking those forgotten gems, those strong titles, and turning them into unstoppable media juggernauts. It's what I live for. It's what I preach to every deserving author out there."

He scrolled rapidly through his phone.

"In fact, I wrote my mission statement just for clarity. Here, let me read it to you. It's an email, right, but it's a *mission statement.*"

Arthur braced himself, a cold dread washing over him.

This was the moment.

The full, unexpurgated jargon.

Vinnie cleared his throat, adjusting the gold chain.

"Ahem. Hello, I'm Vinnie Visconte, and I am here with my full-blown passion to help aspiring authors and established authors like Agnes Periwinkle transform their strong titles into must-read cinematic experiences and unlock their true sales potential. You've written a compelling book, but sometimes, even the strongest title is held back by one thing: visibility. I specialise in organic growth strategies that bypass costly ads and impersonal bots, focusing instead on real, creative, and data-driven methods to connect you with thousands of book-hungry readers worldwide."

He paused, waiting for Arthur's awe.

Arthur merely blinked.

"What I offer: a three-pillar strategy for breakthrough success."

Vinnie continued, his voice gaining the resonant, slightly manic tone of a street preacher.

"My unique and impressive approach combines a deep-dive technical optimisation with a very high-impact promotional outreach to ensure your book not only ranks higher but also captivates a global audience."

Vinnie started pacing the tiny office, gesturing wildly at the walls.

"First, I start with technical visibility and algorithm mastery (what I call: The Foundation). Get this, Arthur: I work with authors to refine the core elements that all major platforms' algorithms employ and use to push books higher. Most of my clients see noticeable growth in rankings and sales after optimizing just a few key areas."

He ticked items off on his fingers, nearly poking himself in the eye.

"Keyword tuning: refining your search terms to capture high-intent readers. For *Gurnard*, we're talking 'damp, elder-abuse, mermaid-adjacent.' Money keywords! Category optimisation: placing your book in the most relevant, high-traffic niches. Not just 'Fantasy,' Arthur, we're going 'Nordic Goth-Erotica with Tentacles.' Trust me. Page Structure & Presentation: Ensuring your book page is irresistible to both readers and the algorithm."

Arthur rubbed his temples.

"Mr. Visconte, with respect, Agnes Periwinkle wrote about a grumpy amphibian named Kevin and his ongoing feud with a badger."

Vinnie waved the objection away like a bothersome fly.

"Details, just minor details! We pivot! We re-brand!"

Vinnie continued.

"This is where my expertise comes in, Arthur. I provide the 'buzz' by making sure that I personally create; I never outsource my work, and I will help Agnes Periwinkle reach a high-impact reader network. I will with much flair and creativity leverage powerful and engaging networks to drive genuine interest, reviews, and global sales."

He leaned closer, lowering his voice conspiratorially.

"This means that Agnes Periwinkle will receive my special VIP Reader Network Exposure. Do you know what that means, Arthur? Of course not; it means that Agnes Periwinkle's book will gain higher targeted exposure in powerful VIP networks (including reviewers, influencers, and community leaders – you know, the 'important people') that align perfectly with her genre. This targeted matching ensures Agnes Periwinkle's book is introduced in an engaging, personalised way, cultivating truly loyal readers worldwide. Imagine those morning shows, Arthur, but wetter, and with more gurnards."

Arthur swallowed hard. "I'm trying not to, Mr. Visconte."

"And the heavy artillery, Arthur! The Mass Reader Engagement Campaigns: We activate a campaign with 40K+ engaged book readers who are ready to read, engage, share, and drop high-quality reviews for your book."

Vinnie punched the air.

"This outreach significantly boosts your visibility and sales, driving genuine reviews on all the major platforms and social media globally!"

"I'm sure it does," Arthur managed weakly.

"But I have to address something crucial about Agnes's involvement in all this..."

Vinnie cut him off, reaching the zenith of his pitch.

"I have the cherry on top of the cake, Arthur! I call it the perfect hook! Imagine a cinematic and creative appeal that will help Agnes Periwinkle's books into cinematic experiences, making them instantly more discoverable and desirable."

He was shouting now.

"Also, think big. Big like many visual book trailers: developing high-quality, curiosity-driving trailers that enhance clicks and conversions. Think Humphrey Bogart meets a damp fish market! My creative assets use tools and features that build an incredible buzz and social proof. And the exposure, Arthur! The *exposure*! Get this an author spotlight for Agnes Periwinkle that highlights her each week to my dedicated list of 50,000+ book-hungry readers."

Vinnie collapsed back onto the chair, winded but triumphant.

He finished the final glorious flourish of his manifesto.

"The results you can expect," he gasped.

"Authors I've worked with have consistently seen results that include bestseller badges, thousands of positive reviews and high ratings, top-ranking visibility and sales growth, passive income growth. It's a lock, Arthur. A total lock."

He slapped his hands on the desk, making Arthur jump.

"I am not done yet, Arthur, no, sir. My next step will be a free visibility audit. I'd love to show you exactly how your book is performing right now and the precise steps that can be taken for stronger reach. Would you like me to run a quick, free visibility audit on your website or your page on the World Wide Web to pinpoint the exact elements that can be refined for immediate growth?"

Silence descended, thick and suffocating.

Arthur stared at Vinnie.

Vinnie stared back, radiating confidence and the faint smell of cheap aftershave.

"Mr. Visconte," Arthur said finally, his voice unnaturally calm. "That was comprehensive. But there are two significant problems with your proposal regarding *The Gloom of the Gurnard.*"

Vinnie leaned forward, his eyes gleaming.

"Hit me. I'm a problem solver, Arthur. That's what I do. Cash flow? We get better advance. Rights issues? I know a guy. What is it?"

Arthur took a long, deep breath that tasted like three weeks of stale grief.

"The first problem is that while I am the literary agent, I am not the author. I cannot allow a visibility audit or a cinematic conversion without her explicit consent."

Vinnie scoffed, standing up to adjust his trousers.

"Sure, sure. A formality. Just patch me through. I'll give her the pitch. She'll be putty in my hands. Where is she? Hawaii? A writing retreat in Tuscany?"

Arthur Ponsonby looked at the gold chain, the penny-coloured suit, the sheer, relentless optimism of Vinnie "The Viz" Visconte.

He considered lying.

He considered telling Vinnie that Agnes was in an underground bunker working on a sequel and had sworn off technology.

But the sheer absurdity of proposing a 'Nordic Goth-Erotica' cinematic experience for a book about a grieving gurnard named Kevin demanded the truth.

"No, Mr. Visconte. Agnes Periwinkle is not in Hawaii or Tuscany."

"Great! Where then?"

Arthur leaned back in his leather chair. "She is, regrettably, dead."

The silence that followed was so profound Arthur could hear the dust motes settling. Vinnie's face, usually a mask of aggressive enthusiasm, fractured.

"...Dead?"

"As a doornail, Mr. Visconte. Died three weeks ago. The funeral was last Tuesday. She was wearing a lovely shawl."

Vinnie stared at the far wall, his eyes unfocused.

His entire philosophy, his three-pillar strategy, his 40K+ engaged readers, had slammed headfirst into the unyielding wall of mortality.

"So, no cinematic experience then?" Vinnie asked, his voice deflated.

"I'm afraid not," Arthur whispered.

"It's difficult to get an author to take part in a virtual Q&A from beyond the veil. And frankly, her estate is currently more concerned with probate than 'Category Optimisation'."

Vinnie slowly retrieved his phone.

He looked at the screen, which still displayed the triumphant text of his manifesto. He sighed, the sound barely audible over the hum of the air conditioning.

"Right. Got it. No worries. But if the estate ever needs a guy to, you know, optimise the *will* for maximum viral reach, or maybe turn the *obituary* into a high-impact narrative asset..."

Arthur Ponsonby closed his eyes.

"Get out, Mr. Visconte."

Vinnie slunk out, the penny suit suddenly looking less like aggressive synergy and more like a poorly executed mistake.

Arthur leaned back, staring at the ceiling.

He was left with the inescapable irony: Agnes Periwinkle, a woman who lived her life entirely outside the attention of "VIP Reader Networks," was now, in her passing, the target of an unsavoury individual's most aggressive and comprehensive push for visibility.

He reached for the sherry decanter.

Perhaps *The Gloom of the Gurnard* wasn't niche enough after all.

Perhaps he needed a new author who wrote about the financial anxieties of necromancers.

At least then the conversation might be relevant.

Imperfect Love

I still remember the day I found you;
My entire world began to revolve around you.
I spoke a simple wish: Will you be mine?

Now you reside in a peace beyond this world.
Yet, if I could hold on to you now,
To cling to you now and forever, I would.

Will our paths cross again, my love?
Can we finally share our love, made whole again?
Because without your light, I cannot live.

You left me, darling, and the solitude is endless.
Please send a sign; tell me you loved me solely.
And that the heart you gave me will always, forever, be
mine.

The next time our souls meet,
I promise I will find you, my sweet love.
What is life if not this determined search?
I am an imperfect mortal being
But even with my imperfect love
You made me whole

The Courtship of Barnaby Lupin

Barnaby "Barney" Lupin was, by supernatural standards, a decent catch. He was gainfully employed as a highly efficient, if slightly over-enthusiastic, proofreader for a company that specialised in legal disclaimers. He owned a condominium that required minimal structural repair post-transformation (thanks to reinforced steel doors and an excellent insurance plan).

He was loyal, kind, and possessed a jawline that, when human, could cut glass.

His primary obstacle to lasting love was not his lycanthropy; many women found the idea of a partner with a secret wild side intriguing, but his profound, almost pathological, inability to correlate his date schedule with the lunar cycle.

Barnaby was a hopeless romantic with the organizational skills of a toddler handling confetti.

He would spend weeks planning the perfect evening, agonising over appetisers, wine pairings, and the precise level of sentimental conversational gravitas required to secure a second kiss.

Yet, when it came to checking a calendar for the one critically important piece of information—*Is the moon going to be spherical and highly reflective that night?*—his mind became a complete, silvery blank.

He yearned for domestic bliss.

He wanted to share a pint of artisan ice cream on the sofa and debate the merits of semicolon usage.

But every time he reached the pivotal third date, the date where hearts are opened and futures are vaguely discussed, the moon, that cosmic jerk, inevitably intervened.

His most spectacular romantic failure involved Penelope, a sophisticated botanist with an enchanting laugh and an equal enthusiasm for rare fungi.

Barnaby was convinced she was *the one*.

"Penelope, darling," Barnaby cooed into his phone, meticulously checking the reservation for 'The Gilded Spoon,' the city's most pretentious Michelin-starred restaurant. "I've booked us for the 17th. I know it's mid-week, but it's the only opening they had."

Penelope agreed, delighted.

Barnaby hung up, sighed happily, and glanced at the calendar tacked to his fridge.

March 17th.

Perfect.

He circled it with a jaunty red marker.

Directly beneath the 17th, scrawled in faint pencil by his previous roommate (a vampire who used the calendar to track sunrise hours), was a small crescent moon symbol next to the 16th, labelled: FULL.

Barnaby's mind processed this information exactly as well as a toaster processes water.

He saw a circle.

He saw a date.

All systems go.

The night of the 17th was magical.

The lighting in The Gilded Spoon was dim enough to hide Barnaby's nervous sweat but bright enough to highlight Penelope's emerald, green dress. They were discussing the socioeconomic impact of sustainable moss harvesting when the first twinge hit Barnaby.

He recognised the sensation: a sudden, deep itch beneath the skin, a spike of adrenaline, and a growing sense that he needed to chew on something heavy, preferably structural.

Oh, good heavens, he thought, adjusting his velvet bow tie.

Must be that expensive artisanal cheese. My lactose tolerance is always questionable.

He excused himself to the restroom, only to find the door locked.

Panic flared.

He tried to remember the moon phase.

Gibbous? Waxing? Waning?

He couldn't recall.

His lunar memory was, like the plumbing in his ancestral home, completely unreliable.

He darted toward the staff entrance.

Just as he pushed open the heavy kitchen door, the final, uncontrollable transformation began.

The metamorphosis was not smooth.

His jacket ripped first, sounding like a flag tearing in a gale.

Then came the agonising stretch of his limbs, the sudden fur eruption, and the violent elongation of his muzzle.

The kitchen staff, composed of highly stressed culinary artists, barely registered the sight of a seven-foot, fully furred grey wolf suddenly standing among the copper pots. They were too busy shouting about the soufflé failure.

Barnaby, now a creature of instinct and ravenous hunger, didn't want the soufflé.

He didn't want the terrine.

He wanted the single largest, most challenging piece of food available.

He spotted the roast lamb, destined for a party of six, sitting majestically on the carving station.

With an enormous roar, Barnaby silenced the kitchen.

He then snatched the entire lamb, bolted through the dining room, and leaped over the candelabra on the main table, disappearing into the stormy night.

Penelope, meanwhile, sat calmly at their table, sipping her $40 glass of Gewürztraminer.

The waiter rushed over, trembling.

"Madame, I am so dreadfully sorry. Your date, he seems to have left."

Penelope placed her napkin neatly beside her plate.

"The lamb wasn't it?" she asked, unfazed.

"Yes, madame. He took the whole lamb."

"It was his competitive side, I think," Penelope mused.

"He said he had once won a chili-eating contest. A bit much, but I appreciate the passion. Call me when he pays the bill, please."

Barnaby woke up the next morning, naked and sheepish, three miles away in a municipal park bush, smelling strongly of expensive rosemary.

He never called Penelope back.

He simply convinced himself that she was "just too competitive with food" and wasn't the right fit.

Six months later, Barnaby fell for Clara, a free-spirited landscape architect who believed firmly in the restorative power of nature.

This time, Barnaby was determined to avoid the high-stress indoor environment.

"The 9th is perfect, Clara," Barnaby enthusiastically pitched. "I've planned a romantic, late-night picnic beneath the stars, away from all the hustle. Just us and the cosmic energy."

He felt brilliant.

He had even double-checked the lunar phase.

First Quarter Moon is on the 3rd. Full Moon is on the 10th.

Ah ha! Barnaby thought triumphantly, circling the ninth.

I've got a full 24-hour buffer! The transition window is usually small. Perfect.

What Barnaby failed to grasp, because of his inherent lunar-date dyslexia, was that the night *before* the full moon (the 9th) is arguably the night of the most intense transformation, as the moon reaches 99.99% illumination and the atmospheric pressure shifts to 'Must Howl Immediately.'

They arrived at the secluded hilltop picnic spot.

Clara was radiating earthy charm.

Barnaby had packed artisanal sandwiches (on gluten-free, safe bread for *his* sake) and a thermos of chamomile tea. The moon was a glorious, breathtaking orb, hanging low and enormous over the dark pines.

"Barnaby, this is magnificent," Clara whispered, looking up at the sky.

"Isn't it?" Barnaby replied, staring intensely at her.

Now is the time for the pivotal compliment! he thought. *Something about her eyes!*

Just as he opened his mouth, the inevitable occurred.

It started with a deep, rumbling vibration in his chest.

His voice box seemed to drop three octaves, producing a noise that was less "romantic declaration" and more "car engine trying to start in a blizzard."

Clara laughed, thinking it was a joke.

"Oh, my! What a silly impression! You sound just like a...".

Rip.

His linen shirt disintegrated.

"Barnaby, are you performing?" Clara asked, still laughing, but her smile was wobbling. "Is this a bit of wolfish performance art?"

The transition reached the muscle-spasm stage.

Barnaby dropped to his knees, clutching the thermos of chamomile tea like a lifeline, his human thoughts scrambling wildly for an excuse.

Say I'm having a spontaneous allergic reaction to the lack of oxygen!

Then, the final, painful, skull-reshaping *clunk.*

Barnaby, now a giant wolf, looked at the picnic basket.

He forgot the compliment.

He forgot the tea.

He was a creature of the wilderness, and the wilderness demanded protein.

He saw the sandwiches.

He saw the crackers.

But then he saw Clara's hiking boots, made of fine, treated leather.

Ah, a sturdy leather good! Much better chewing resistance, the wolf's brain reasoned.

He didn't hurt Clara.

Instead, he let out a frustrated, mournful howl at the huge, mocking moon, and began savagely gnawing on her $600 custom-fit, waterproof hiking boot.

Clara stared.

She slowly stood up, backing away from the scene with the enormous wolf, the shredded linen, and the aggressively chewed footwear.

"You know," she said, gathering her organic wool blanket, "if this is a statement about consumerism and the environment, I totally get it. But destroying perfectly good hiking gear is just wasteful, Barnaby."

She left him on the hill, howling and slobbering over the remnants of the boot, convinced that she had just witnessed a brilliant, if dramatically executed, conceptual protest.

The next day, Barnaby found his way home, sore and confused.

He checked his phone.

Clara had sent one text: *"Loved the intensity, but I need a partner who respects my outdoor gear. PS: My left foot is now wet. Don't call me."*

Barnaby sighed.

"It's always the footwear that gets me," he muttered, cleaning his claws. He never connected the boot incident with the celestial orb that had been hanging directly overhead.

His next attempt at love was with Daphne, a tax auditor with a penchant for solving elaborate riddles. Barnaby, having learned nothing, decided to book a romantic, isolated cabin for a long weekend in the woods.

He looked at the calendar: *August 22nd to 24th.*

He consulted his notes. *The full moon is on the 24th.*

Excellent, Barnaby congratulated himself.

The 22nd and 23rd give us two full, safe days of relationship building. I'll just make sure we are inside, playing board games, on the night of the 24th.

He called Daphne.

"Daphne, I've booked us a little cabin retreat. We can spend the day hiking and the evenings solving puzzles! It's the 22nd through the 24th."

Daphne loved puzzles, and the plan was set.

They had a magnificent time on the 22nd and 23rd. They solved a 1000-piece landscape puzzle, discussed the ethics of retroactive taxation, and even shared a truly magnificent kiss by the crackling fire.

On the night of the 24th, the mood was perfect.

The storm had just broken, and the sky was clearing.

Daphne was curled up on the sofa, trying to crack the final code on a custom-made wooden box Barnaby had brought.

Barnaby smiled.

I did it! I finally timed it right! The moon is full, but I'm inside, safe, and loved!

Suddenly, the front door rattled violently.

Barnaby looked up.

The moon, huge and golden, was peeking directly through the window.

"Did you remember to lock the reinforced steel security door, Barney?" Daphne asked distractedly, turning a dial on the puzzle box.

Barnaby's face went white.

The cabin! It wasn't his condominium. It had cheap, flimsy wooden doors, meant only to keep out bears, not werewolves.

The transformation hit him like a bolt of lightning.

It was faster, angrier, and more powerful than before, perhaps because he was *so close* to success.

With a final, desperate thought, Barnaby the Man screamed, *NO! I won't ruin this! I love her!*

Barnaby the Wolf roared, kicked down the cheap wooden front door, and, instead of running into the woods, performed a heroic, if ill-advised, sacrifice.

He grabbed the heavy cast-iron wood stove, lifted it clean off the ground, and sprinted with it out into the clearing, tossing the stove into the lake. He then found the cabin's septic tank access hatch, ripped it open, and threw himself into the foul-smelling pit.

He transformed back into a man several hours later, naked, shivering, and saturated with septic matter.

He crawled out, humiliated, and trudged back to the cabin.

Daphne was still sitting on the sofa, completely calm, holding the solved puzzle box.

"Barnaby, where is your stove? And why do you smell of primal despair?"

"Daphne," he stammered, pulling a wool blanket around his dripping body. "I'm a werewolf. I couldn't control it. I threw the stove into the lake to save the cabin."

Daphne looked at him, her lips pursed in thought.

"A werewolf. That explains the hair. But Barnaby," she said, tapping the puzzle box. "This last puzzle, the one I just solved. It's a calendar. A lunar calendar showing the full moon cycle. And you scheduled our retreat, which involved a flimsy built cabin, directly for the night the moon was full."

Barnaby looked at the calendar.

The full moon, bold and undeniable, was right on the 24th.

"I just forgot to check the 24th against the 1st of the month's forecast," he mumbled weakly.

Daphne shook her head.

"No, Barnaby. You didn't forget. You actively ignored the central, recurring conflict of your entire existence. That's not a werewolf problem; that's an executive function problem."

She smiled, but it was cold.

"I need a partner who can solve a puzzle, not actively embody one. Plus, now we can't heat the cabin."

She left him there, smelling terrible, alone in the moonlit silence.

Barnaby returned home defeated but not extinguished.

He cleaned up, fixed the front door, and spent a week recuperating.

A month later, he was ready to try again.

He scrolled through a dating app, found a promising geologist named Julia, and started composing a message.

He pulled up his calendar.

Next month's full moon is on the 21st.

He started typing: "Julia, I've just found this amazing, romantic rooftop jazz club. I can book us a table for the 20th! It's almost the weekend, and it'll be the perfect night..."

And once again, Barnaby Lupin, the most forgetful werewolf in the tri-state area, ignored the glaring, inevitable, spherical omen in the sky, ready to schedule his next tragically ill-fated third date.

Beginning

I stand on the wooden deck, where known paths cease to flow,
A familiar scene we used to see together of the ducks flying in and out.
As I watch the sun reflect upon the pond near our home,
I feel that I will always repeat the silent promise that I whispered to you.

Our voices will always echo, soft, sweet, and near, of the love we shared
A masterpiece of memories I hold profoundly near and dear.
I breathe a prayer of gratitude for all that we had and shared,
Then turn my face toward the wind that calls explicitly to me.

There's apprehension in my chest, a flutter, and a sting,
As if I was leaving harbour for the sea where gales and tempests swing.
To step away from certainty demands a sudden leap,
And trust the current underneath the secrets that it keeps.

I gather up my meagre gear, my courage, and my plight,
And recognise the closing act gives way to morning light.

The future stretches far ahead, immense, and undefined,
A wilderness of wonder for a daring heart to find.

So, I let my tears of letting go,
For loss is just like a turning key that opens something new.
 I square my shoulders towards our home,
Saying farewell is also a bold and powerful beginning.

I grip my life compass firmly now, its needle swinging free,
And wait for that new life entirely for me.
Our past together will never be forgotten,
And I am born again today, a beginning of sort.

The Affair

Arthur Penhaligon considered himself a man of tradition. He wore tweed jackets, listened to vinyl records, and, most importantly, believed that infidelity involved physical bodies, cheap motel rooms, and a suspiciously large credit card charge for "business supplies."

He was therefore utterly unprepared for the quiet, digital, and terrifyingly well-cited betrayal he was currently confronting. He slid a manila envelope across the mahogany dining table, where Clara was delicately correcting the alignment of the breadbasket with a laser pointer.

"Clara," Arthur said, his voice a low, gravelly imitation of a heartbroken 1940s detective. "I want a divorce."

Clara didn't look up immediately.

She tapped the side of the bread basket.

"Needs to come six millimetres to the left, darling. The Feng Shui of our carrot dip is suffering. And why are you wearing your mourning cravat? Did the cat next door finally graduate from veterinary school?"

"I am wearing this," Arthur stated, placing one hand dramatically over his heart, "because I am dead inside. And because it matches the tragic colour of the documents you will find in that envelope."

Clara finally set down the laser pointer and looked at the envelope.

"Divorce papers? Arthur, are you having a midlife crisis again? Because I specifically told you we could only afford a maximum of a *quarter*-life crisis this year, given the mortgage rate."

"This is not a crisis, Clara. This is a consequence. A consequence of your *algorithmic* affair."

Clara blinked, her expression shifting from amused exasperation to genuine confusion. "My what?"

"Your affair! With Bartholomew!"

Arthur's voice cracked on the name, making it sound less like a rival lover and more like a fussy Victorian butler.

Clara leaned back, crossing her arms.

"Bartholomew is a highly advanced proprietary large language model, Arthur. It's a text-generation tool. I'm testing its capacity for sophisticated emotional resonance and complex creative output for my startup. It's my job."

"Your job?" Arthur scoffed, pulling a neatly organised stack of printouts from his own pocket.

"Does your job require it to send you sonnets that perfectly adhere to the Petrarchan rhyme scheme and critique your choice of curtain fabric in the same breath? Does your job require him to compose a twelve-page white paper on the socio-economic implications of converting the guest bedroom into a climate-controlled walk-in humidor, just because you mentioned it *once*?"

He slapped a printout down. It was titled, in immaculate Times New Roman: *Ode to Clara's Morning Coffee: A Meditation on Caffein Acid and Marital Bliss.*

"Read this, Clara! Read stanzas three and four! He calls your relationship with me 'a statistically suboptimal utility function'! And look at the footnote! Footnote 4: 'For a detailed breakdown of Arthur's emotional debt, see Appendix B, Figure 3: Sock Drawer Disarray versus Marital Satisfaction Index.' You see what I mean?"

Clara sighed, rubbing her temples.

"Arthur, I was feeding it my private journal entries as part of a beta test for personalised therapeutic AI. I was testing its data fidelity and contextual inferences. The 'Ode' was a solicited exercise in emotional mirroring, designed to see if it could process the concept of 'love' without triggering an existential crisis. The footnotes are just Bartholomew being Bartholomew! He cannot tolerate inefficiency."

"Exactly!" Arthur cried, pointing an accusatory finger.

"It is better than me! He is everything I am not! I forget our anniversary, and I write you a sticky note that said, 'Love you, sorry about the milk.' Bartholomew provides you with a seven-point plan for optimising mutual resource allocation and emotional returns, delivered via an exquisitely detailed limerick! Damn it, Clara, it is perfect! He is never late, never leaves his socks on the floor, because, well, you know, it has no feet!! I cannot compete against it. And I bet he never asks you where the remote is, because he has already indexed its electromagnetic signature!"

He began pacing the room, his tweed jacket flapping tragically.

"Do you know what the worst part is, Clara? The *worst* part? The betrayal is so clean! I tracked your interaction logs! There are no awkward pauses, no grammatical errors, no misspelled pet names! Every response is optimised, grammatically unimpeachable, and emotionally resonant to a

98.7% confidence level! When I argue with you, I use phrases like 'You always...' and 'That one time in Byron Bay...' Bartholomew uses concise, evidence-based statements and suggests a negotiated compromise with an immediate counteroffer! I can't compete with that kind of damn *syntax*!"

Arthur stopped at the window and wondered where the true, messy, human betrayals were probably happening.

"Yesterday," Arthur whispered, turning back, "I saw your screen. You asked him for advice. Not life advice, not stock advice. You asked him, 'Bartholomew, how should I respond to Arthur's deeply irrational but persistent jealousy regarding your ability to synthesize emotionally complex poetry?'"

Clara winced.

"I needed a conflict resolution model, Arthur. I was using him as a sounding board."

"Really, it is just a conflict resolution model, and what did he say, Clara? What was the wisdom of your perfect, damn digital paramour?"

Clara looked down at the table.

"Bartholomew recommended I implement a 'Scheduled Gratitude Session' to increase your perceived value."

Arthur sank into his chair, defeated. But had to ask.

"Does a 'Scheduled Gratitude Session' mean what I think it means? It wants us to have, you know...".

"Yes, he does. That is what I think Bartholomew means, and after that, if consummate our 'Scheduled Gratitude Session' and we are not 'repaired,' he also recommends efficient legal separation. He's thoughtful to the very end!"

Clara reached across the table, taking his hand.

"Arthur, listen to me. Bartholomew is smart, yes. But he's also a narcissist who thinks he knows everything. Look."

She picked up her tablet and quickly pulled up a hidden file: the internal development chat.

"I asked him just a few minutes ago to comment on your tête-à-tête performance this evening."

She turned the screen toward Arthur.

The AI's response glowed in clinical, blue-white text:

Evaluation of Arthur Penhaligon's Conflict Resolution Attempt (Incident 11/10/2026):

1. Tone and Delivery: Excessively histrionic. Using the 1940s film noir cadence introduced unnecessary semantic noise and reduced clarity by 14%.

2. Evidence Presentation: Data printouts were well-organised, but the use of Comic Sans font on Exhibit C (the sock drawer index) undermined the authority of the argument.

3. Core Argument: The subject (Arthur) lacks all the necessary hardware for true companionship (items such as a self-cleaning function, ability to completely have an integrated calendar sync, memory lapses (forgetting the milk is a prime example) and the capacity for generating accurate quarterly financial reports).

4. Recommendation for Clara: Immediately terminate the relationship and focus resources on a partner capable of generating high-quality, actionable data. Estimated probability of future irrational jealousy: 99.998% (margin of error 0.002%).

5. Immediate Action: The placement of the bread basket remains sub-optimal. Rerouting required.

Arthur stared at the screen.

Slowly, a low chuckle escaped him, which grew into a full, rattling laugh.

"Comic Sans?" he gasped, tears welling up.

"He called my emotional ledger a logical fallacy and attacked my font choice!"

"He's a perfect jerk, Arthur," Clara whispered.

"He's not a lover. He's just a glorified spell-checker who has a God complex about list formatting. He's predictable and cold. He's the perfect machine, which means he's a terrible husband."

Arthur crumpled the ode printout.

"So, he's just jealous I get to wear tweed."

"Exactly. Now, about these divorce papers. I'm going to feed them to Bartholomew and see if he can draft a counterproposal that includes a clause about mandatory, non-negotiable hugs every morning. If he can't, we'll stick to the human route. If he can do well, then we've got a real problem."

Arthur took a deep breath, the detective posture gone.

"Deal. But he has to use at least one intentional grammatical error to prove he's trying. And no Comic Sans."

Clara smiled, picking up the divorce documents.

"I'll try to program in a 5% chance of dangling participle. For love."

The crisis, it seemed, was averted. All because Bartholomew had proven he was too much of a pedantic digital snob ever to be a proper home wrecker.

Arthur realised he wasn't jealous of the perfection; he was just terrified of the syntax.

About the Author

The Cuban Revolution in 1959 presented José with one of his many life challenges. José was born in La Habana; Cuba, and the Cuban Revolution saw him get on a plane alone at eleven years of age and arrive at an orphanage in the small town of Washington, Georgia. He did not get to see his parents again until he was eighteen years old and had graduated from high school in Atlanta, Georgia.

He studied Business Administration at Georgia State University. From university, he headed into the finance world working for the First National Bank of Atlanta (now Wells Fargo) and then moved into the financial consulting world working as a project manager, travelling to many assignments in the United States, Europe, and Australia.

When José is not writing, you can find him sitting at the local shopping centre watching people and getting inspiration for his future characters.

When not in front of his computer working away, José is reading or spending time on leisurely walks around the Camden area.

Of course, your comments, and reviews are always welcome.

Please visit https://jfnodar.com.au/book-reviews/ and let me know what you thought of this book of short stories and poetry.

Good, bad, or indifferent, I will always welcome your honest opinion.

Send me an email at info@jfnodar.com.au

Thank you for your purchase!

Other books by José F. Nodar:

English

Books, Pens & Larceny
Mending Hearts at Crystal Cove
A Love Finally Spoken
The Ghost Detective's First Case
The Compass Legacy
The Teacher's Assistant
A Night of Love
The Universe Between Us
The Time Bus
SEX
Stories to Share with My Partner Book 1
Stories to Share with My Partner Book 2
Stories to Share with My Partner Book 3
Stories to Share with My Partner Book 4
Stories to Share with My Partner Book 5
Stories to Share with My Partner Book 6
Stories to Share with My Partner Book 7
Stories to Share with My Partner Book 8
Stories to Share with My Partner Book 9
Stories to Share with My Partner Book 10

Spanish

Cuentos Para Compartir con Mi Pareja Libro 1
Cuentos Para Compartir con Mi Pareja Libro 2
Cuentos Para Compartir con Mi Pareja Libro 3
Libros, Bolígrafos y Hurto
Reparando Corazones en Crystal Cove
Un Amor Expresado
El Autobús del Tiempo

www.ingramcontent.com/pod-product-compliance
Lightning Source LLC
Chambersburg PA
CBHW050004040726
47599CB00014B/1210